THE CHERRY VALLEY MIDDLE SCHOOL NEWS

DEAR KNOW-IT-ALL

★ ★ ★

READ ALL ABOUT IT!

Simon Spotlight

New York   London   Toronto   Sydney   New Delhi

This book is a work of fiction. Any references to historical events, real people, or real locales are used fictitiously. Other names, characters, places, and incidents are the product of the author's imagination, and any resemblance to actual events or locales or persons, living or dead, is entirely coincidental.

SIMON SPOTLIGHT
An imprint of Simon & Schuster Children's Publishing Division
1230 Avenue of the Americas, New York, New York 10020
Copyright © 2012 by Simon & Schuster, Inc. All rights reserved, including the right of reproduction in whole or in part in any form.
SIMON SPOTLIGHT and colophon are registered trademarks of Simon & Schuster, Inc.
Text by Elizabeth Doyle Carey
Designed by Laura L. DiSiena

For information about special discounts for bulk purchases, please contact Simon & Schuster Special Sales at 1-866-506-1949 or business@simonandschuster.com.
Manufactured in the United States of America 0413 OFF
First Edition 10 9 8 7 6 5 4 3 2 1
ISBN 978-1-4424-9697-2 (pbk)
ISBN 978-1-4424-5382-1 (hc)
ISBN 978-1-4424-4403-4 (eBook)
Library of Congress Control Number 2011943077

Chapter 1

MARTONE SAYS SCHOOL YEAR OFF TO GOOD START!

★ ★ ★

Do you need to know everything about everything? I do. I'm kind of a newshound, which is what my parents call me. My sister, Allie, calls me weird. She's only interested in news about celebrities and certain cute guys in her class. But I am all about *real* news and how to get it. According to my mom, ever since I could talk, all I've done is ask questions. Now that I'm older, asking questions is a habit (sometimes a bad one). The hard part for me is stopping to listen to the answer, because as soon as someone begins to answer, I'm already forming the next question in my mind! This is okay, though, because I want to be a journalist when I grow up, and journalists need to ask lots of questions.

The best thing *ever* happened to me this summer (sorry, sometimes I switch gears fast too!). My aunt Louisa, who is a reporter, and my idol, gave me the most amazing birthday present: one week at a *sleepaway* writing camp! My best friend, Hailey, goes to sports camp, and she thought writing camp sounded sooooo boring, but it wasn't at all. And the best part was you got to pick what kind of writing you focused on while you were there. I picked journalism, of course. My teacher was this cool old guy named Mr. Bloom, who'd been the international news desk editor for the *New York Times*. He was old, but he was really smart, and he taught me a ton about journalism.

Journalism is reporting and writing what is going on in the world around you, near and far, and it is really fun because you get to ask lots of questions and learn lots of facts! Every story you write has to answer these questions: What? Who? Where? When? Why? And how?

Like if I were reporting a story about myself right now, I'd write:

Monday, September 7

MARTONE OFF TO A GREAT START!

Samantha Martone headed back to Cherry Valley Middle School today for her first day of school. When her alarm rang at 6:30 a.m., she hopped out of bed to check all the blogs and news websites she likes to read first thing every morning. After showering and drying her long brown hair, she dressed with care, "Because first impressions matter," says Martone.

At school Martone was thrilled to discover that both her best friend since kindergarten, Hailey Jones, *and* her major crush, Michael Lawrence, would be in her homeroom this year.

During lunch hour, Samantha visited the office of the *Cherry Valley Voice*, the school newspaper, to sign up as a reporter again with Mr. Trigg, the *Voice*'s faculty supervisor. (Shh! Don't tell: Martone would like to be the editor in chief of the *Cherry Valley Voice* next year!) Samantha Martone is looking forward to another great year at Cherry Valley Middle School. "Cherry Valley rules!" said Ms. Martone.

Isn't that funny? It sounds like real news, right? Pretty much when you call people by their last names, it makes things sound official. That's just one of the things I've learned about journalism during the past year.

My favorite thing is writing headlines. I write headlines in my mind all day long. Like, right now I'm on my way home from school. In just one more suburban block (left on Buttermilk Lane), I will reach number seventeen, where I live, and the headline will be ***Martone Home, Shares Day with Mom.*** Later it might be ***Martone Kids Riot, Meatloaf Again!*** or ***Reality Sets In as Homework Pile Is Revealed.*** Actually, that one might be too long. I usually like my headlines to be catchier than that ("pithy" is the word Mr. Trigg uses), but you get the idea.

"Mom!" I yelled as I entered the house. We live in a split-level so she could have been upstairs or down. "Mom!"

"In the den, honey!"

I clomped down a level and found her at her desk.

"Hi! How was it?" she asked with a grin. My mom is a freelance bookkeeper and she had a project spread out all across her work area.

"What's that?" I asked, peering over her

shoulder. "Who's it for? Why do you have so many ledgers? Hey, when did you—"

"Stop!" My mom held her hand up in front like a crossing guard. It's a sign we agreed on for when I'm asking too many questions and not listening enough, which drives her crazy. "Sit," she commanded with a smile.

I sat. I was smiling too.

"Hi, honey," she said, starting over.

"Hi, Mom." I tried hard to be quiet and not ask any questions for a second. At writing camp they said journalists have to know how to be quiet, too, because sometimes the best information isn't even spoken aloud. Plus, being a good reporter means you have to be a good listener, too.

"How was your day?" she asked.

I told her all about homeroom and how cute Michael Lawrence looks with a tan and how great it was to see Hailey, who'd only gotten back from camp a week earlier and was coming over in an hour to do homework (yes, we have homework already!), and how I'd signed up for the school paper again and I was thinking of trying out for the soccer team with Hailey, and how we have a new curriculum, and what was for lunch and . . . everything.

"It sounds wonderful!" said my mom. "What a great day!"

I was happy too. It *had* been a great day. Now it was my turn to listen while my mom talked.

"In brief, I am working on a project for a new client, and they have three retail stores, so three accounts. Their old bookkeeper wrote everything by hand in ledgers, so I'm putting everything into computer files for them. It's fun."

"Good!" I said, though I was fibbing. I truly cannot imagine how bookkeeping is any fun, but it's important to make people feel good about the work they do so that they will continue to give you information that you might need for a story. That's another piece of advice I learned at camp. Not that I had to worry about Mom withholding information, but it was good practice anyway.

My mom hadn't finished. "But more importantly, Mr. Trigg called from school right before you got here. He asked you to call him back. Here's his direct extension." My mom handed me a piece of paper.

"Why was he calling?" I asked. I took the slip of paper and studied it as if it might contain more information, but all it had was the number. I didn't like the idea of a call from a teacher. That didn't sound good. Maybe he was kicking me off the paper! Maybe he thought my writing wasn't good enough! Now I'll never stand a chance to be editor in chief. . . . "What did he say?" I asked.

My mom shrugged. "Give him a call," she said. "Use the phone in the kitchen so I can finish up here."

I stood up and, still staring at the number in my hand, trudged up the stairs and across the hall to the kitchen. I hesitated to pick up the phone and dial. Usually I love making phone calls. I'll call anyone! I'm never shy on the phone. But when it's something about *me* . . . well.

Martone Axed by Trigg, I thought. But no, he wouldn't call me at home for that. I shook my head, squared my shoulders, and dialed the phone.

"Hello?" It was Mr. Trigg. Gosh, he was a fast answerer.

"Hi, Mr. Trigg. . . . It's Sam Martone. Uh. You called me?"

"Samantha! Thank you for calling me back so promptly! I have a very important question for you and I couldn't ask it today at school because there were too many people around. Too many newshounds!" He laughed his big guffaw. Mr. Trigg is British and kind of a nerd, but I like him. He thinks grammar and vocabulary are the most important things on Earth. Also impartiality. He used to be a journalist in London, or as he would say, a "journo."

I giggled nervously. "Okay," I said. "What's up?"

Mr. Trigg collected himself. "Samantha, I will cut to the chase. Would you like to be our Know-It-All this year?"

My jaw dropped. Dear Know-It-All is the most important column in our school paper! It's kind of like Dear Abby, where kids write in anonymously about their problems, and the Know-It-All answers. And no matter what is on the front page of the paper, Dear Know-It-All is the first thing all the kids read when the paper comes out, and it is the thing people talk about the most. Whoever writes it each year is a mystery. No one has ever guessed who it is. I actually thought Mr. Trigg himself might be the writer, but apparently not. Anyway, me? Know-It-All? But I don't know anything!

"Uh . . . oh my gosh. Wow! Mr. Trigg! That is so major. I don't know what to say!" I felt scared, flattered, excited, inspired . . . everything all at once! This was huge.

"Well, I hope you will say yes!" said Mr. Trigg.

It hadn't occurred to me to say no. I mean, why would I say no? Okay, I didn't know a lot about a lot of things. Like boys, for instance. And there were always a lot of letters about boys. But I could learn. Isn't that what a journalist does? Investigate? Research? Figure it out? Plus, if I did a really good job, maybe it would help me get to the editor in chief position, which is what I really, really wanted for next year.

I had to accept. "Well . . . then, yes! Okay. Thank you! I'd love to!" I laughed nervously.

I couldn't wait to tell my friends.

"Excellent. I will e-mail you the guidelines we use for the column and I will collect the student letters each week. I am happy to help you pick an appropriate one for each issue, and then you will e-mail me your written response, which I need to approve. It will all be kept strictly confidential. You understand that no one must know your identity, right, Samantha?"

"Right." I nodded. Wait, I can't even tell *Hailey*? I thought. Really? Hailey could keep a secret. . . .

"Not even your best friend," continued Mr. Trigg, as if he was reading my mind.

Oh well, that answers that question. "Okay," I agreed. I hadn't thought about that. I tell Hailey everything. This could be harder than I thought.

"Confidentiality is the most important part of the job. Loose lips sink ships!" He guffawed again. Mr. Trigg is a World War II buff and I think that line comes from the war or something. "I spoke to your mother, of course, but she assures me that our secret is safe with her!"

Whew, I thought. At least Mom knows. But Mom always said we didn't have secrets in our family. I wondered if she would tell Allie. I loved the idea that we had a secret from Allie.

"All right! Thanks, Mr. Trigg."

"Righty-ho, Samantha. I will e-mail you with utmost alacrity! So long!"

"Bye." I hung up the phone, then whipped out the notebook and pencil that I carry with me everywhere. I wrote "Dear Know-It-All, by Samantha Martone."

It looked amazing. But then I crossed it out really dark so no one could ever read it. I just needed to get it out of my system. I closed the notebook, stashed it and the pencil back in my pocket, and just spaced out for a second in the kitchen.

Wow. Me? Know-It-All?

Really?

Chapter 2

BEST FRIENDS REUNITE

The front door banged open while I was eating a snack and thinking about my new column.

"Helloooo!" It was Hailey.

"Hail-ooooo, Hailey! In the kitchen!" I yelled. Darn, I wished I could tell her!

"Hi, honey!" my mom called from her office.

"Hi, Mrs. M.!" Hailey yelled back.

A second later my best friend, Hailey Jones, popped her head into the kitchen doorway. "What's up, sister?" she said with a grin.

Hailey and I could not look less alike. I have long dark brown hair and she has bright blond short hair. (A "pixie cut" is what she calls it.) I am tall and she is . . . well, not tall. She's not totally short but sometimes people do mistake her for a fourth grader, which drives her crazy and makes me laugh. Hailey is really muscle-y and coordinated, and I am pretty much a weak klutz. We both have a lot of energy, but mine is more for talking and hers is more for doing, if you know what I mean. I think it's because she has two older brothers and she was always chasing them around and playing sports with them and stuff. Whereas at my house, my older sister, Allie, and I talk, talk, talk and read, read, read. (And sometimes fight, fight, fight!)

Hailey hopped on to the stool next to me. She propped her head on her hand and looked at what I was eating. I am always hungry and always eating. Hailey isn't that big of an eater, but her mom is such a health-food nut that when Hailey comes to our house she sometimes goes crazy on our junk food—even the stuff that isn't that junky to most people, like white bread and regular milk. It's like she has to just have it when she gets the chance, because the opportunity might not come along again soon.

"Want some?" I asked, pushing the peanut-buttered English muffin toward her.

She scrunched up her nose. "Nah. So what did you think?"

"About today? Pretty good," I replied. "What about you?"

"Yeah, me too. Pretty good," said Hailey, nodding. "Are you going to try out for soccer with me this year, or what?" she asked, grabbing the English muffin and taking a bite after all. She chewed quickly and watched me for my response about soccer. This was an ongoing battle between us. I don't know why Hailey even has to try out. She was the star center last year!

I sighed. "Maybe," I said.

"You always say that!" she cried, punching me in the arm.

"Ow." I looked down at my arm and brushed off some imaginary crumbs, then I looked back at her. "Physical violence never solves anything," I said, mimicking my mother. It's one of her big lines.

"Yes it does!" said Hailey through a mouth full of peanut butter.

"'Girl Maimed by Best Friend,'" I said. "How does that sound, huh?"

"Great!" said Hailey wickedly. "Now come on. This is the year. Come with me and just go for it! It would be so much more fun if we did it together!"

Even though Hailey is a doer and I am a watcher, we get along because Hailey gets me to try new things, which is good. Mom calls it "pulling me out of my comfort zone." I guess it's good but I like my comfort zone. It's comfortable. "When is it?" I asked, thinking it might be a good story to cover for the paper: *Soccer Hopefuls Give It Their All*.

"Tomorrow, Wednesday, and Thursday."

I pretended to consider it. "I'll come tomorrow," I said finally.

"You will?!" Hailey threw her arms around me. "Yay! I love you!"

"Down girl!" I said, laughing. "I'm not trying out. Just reporting." I could pitch a story to the sports section.

Hailey unhugged me and did a fake pout. "Now I hate you." She crossed her arms.

"I hate you too, but not forever. What else about today? Who's in your English section with you?"

"Language arts," Hailey said, correcting me.

Since we have a new curriculum this year, all the subjects have fancy new names. It's really confusing.

"Right! Language arts," I said to correct myself.

"More like language farts," said Hailey, cracking herself up. The girl really does not like to read or write.

Hailey moved restlessly around the room, picking things up and putting them back down. "So who are the hotties this year?" she asked.

"Oh, the usual. Looking better than ever with that awesome tan." I didn't even need to say his name. Michael Lawrence had been my crush for years. Really since I met him. The only bummer is that I met him in kindergarten when a onetime paste-eating experiment earned me the nickname Pasty (I thought it was frosting! I swear!). He still calls me that on a regular basis, and it makes me want to die. If he weren't so cute, I'd have Hailey punch him for me.

"Yeah," she said. "He looks good."

"Who do you like?" I asked, not expecting an answer. Hailey never liked anyone real. Most of her crushes were on famous guys.

"Oh . . . I don't know. Maybe I'll like someone this year," she said.

I perked up, my journalist senses tingling. "Like who?" I pressed.

"Oh, I don't know. I just think . . . I think it's time I liked someone," she said.

I nodded and grinned. "Interesting. And when do you think this liking will begin?"

"Shut up," said Hailey. "I don't need to be interviewed."

I ignored her. "What about Jeff Perry?" Jeff Perry is one of Michael's best friends and he's pretty cute too. They play baseball together in the spring, and he's a photographer on the *Voice*. Also, he's not too tall; that would be another plus for Hailey.

Hailey shrugged. "Maybe him."

I tapped my front tooth thoughtfully. "How are you going to go about all this? Are you going to audition boys? Make them try out?"

Hailey glared at me and I heard the front door open again, then shut.

"Allie?" I heard my mom call.

"Hi!" replied my older sister, Allie. I didn't hear any footsteps. That meant Allie was in the middle of texting someone and had stopped dead in her tracks. I looked at Hailey and rolled my eyes.

Allie is in the tenth grade, and texting and the Internet are her life. She hardly communicates in real life anymore; it's all online. Posting, texting, e-mailing links, uploading photos, downloading videos—it's all she does. On the plus side, she's the student coordinator for the high school website, which is a pretty big job, so at least she's getting some kind of recognition out of all this. It's just annoying to be around her because she's always distracted. I know one day I'll see a headline in the one of those wacky grocery store newspapers, like *Freakish Girl Grows Giant Thumbs: Texting to Blame* or something like that, and it will be Allie.

Hailey, of course, finds Allie fascinating, because she doesn't have an older sister. She refused to roll her eyes back at me.

Allie appeared in the doorway, still texting.

"OMG!" I said in a fake high-pitched voice. "TTYL! XOXO!"

Allie didn't even look up. Just finished her typing, laughing a little at something she was writing, and then clicked her phone shut and looked up. It was like she was re-entering the atmosphere, and it took her a minute to adjust and realize we were there.

"Hi, Allie," said Hailey shyly.

"Hey, Hails," said Allie. She knew Hailey worshiped her and she loved it. "Hey, little sis," she said. "How was the first day of kindergarten?"

"We're in middle school," Hailey corrected her respectfully.

"Hailey." I groaned. "She knows. She's just torturing us."

Allie flashed us a grin and Hailey laughed.

"Oh, funny. Good one," Hailey said.

Now I rolled my eyes again.

Allie can be great when she feels like it. She's very pretty, tall, and really fit, with long, wavy sandy blond hair ("popular girl hair" is what my friends called it in grade school). She's smart and has cool friends and is a good dresser. But she can also be really mean. Like, right when you think she's your friend, she lashes out at you or cuts you dead or rats you out. This is only if you're her sister, of course. If you're her friend, she treats you like gold.

"Any new hotties?" she asked, opening the

fridge and staring blankly inside.

"Nah," I said.

"Still pining away for ML?" She looked at me with a grin and winked at Hailey.

Hailey laughed and her cheeks turned pink.

Allie did a double take. "Wait, *you* like him, *too*?" Allie said in shock.

Hailey looked mortified. "Me? What? No!" She shook her head vehemently.

Allie looked at her suspiciously, then laughed. "There's gotta be more than one cute guy in middle school."

I nodded, though I couldn't think of anyone else. (Even Jeff Perry didn't count.) Was Allie just trying to stir up trouble?

"How's Trigger?" Allie asked, changing the subject. Allie had been on the school paper too, but it wasn't her passion. She liked Mr. Trigg though.

"He's good. He . . ." *Oh my goodness!* (Or should I say OMG!) I had nearly blurted out that he had called me!

"He what?" she pressed, staring at me quizzically. Allie has major radar for someone who spends all her time plugged into electronics. She'd actually make a great reporter.

"He's the same old, same old," I said, fake laughing and shaking my head from side to side. "That guy!"

Allie looked at me for an extra minute but I had scrambled her radar. Luckily, just then her phone chirped and I was dead to her anyway.

She pulled it out and left the room.

"Homework?" I said to Hailey.

"Okay. Can you help me with language farts?" I always help Hailey with her English homework. It's a ritual. She's pretty dyslexic and hates reading and writing because it takes her so long.

"Sure, if you help me with math."

As we went up the stairs to my room an overwhelming wave of frustration washed over me. I was dying to tell Hailey about Know-It-All, and Allie too, but I couldn't do it. It made me feel lonely.

I wished I could tell Michael Lawrence. I think it would impress him.

But he'd probably just say, "Way to go, Pasty."

Chapter 3

GIRL SUES CLASSMATE FOR HARASSMENT— THEN MARRIES HIM!

★ ★ ★

It felt great to be back in the newsroom. The energy, the deadlines, the smell of toner. I always felt excited when we were putting together the paper.

"Let's get some man-on-the-street reactions . . ." our editor in chief was saying. "Interview some parents . . . Jeff, you'll get out and take photos . . ."

We were having a staff meeting to plan out the first issue of the school paper. It comes out every other week, so we have a good lead time to research the articles, write them, file them (which means turn them in), have them edited and laid out, and then put the paper to bed (which means get the final, final version off to the printer). Our editor in chief is Susannah Johnson, who is in eighth grade.

She is extremely smart and very cool, and she is also captain of the field hockey team.

This year we were assigned stories each week, and I had been assigned to report and write a lead article about the new curriculum changes at the school. Lead articles are on the front page, usually "above the fold," which is what newspapers call the top half of the front page. It's where the most important news goes, and for a reporter, it's an honor to have your work placed there. It was shaping up to be a great year for me at the paper.

Susannah and Mr. Trigg and I were working out everything the curriculum story should contain, or as Mr. Trigg said, "hitting all the angles." I learned that at writing camp. To be a good journalist you have to be able to look at something from all different angles so you aren't just reporting on one side of the story.

"Why don't you talk to two or three parents as part of the man-on-the-street interviews, and then call Mrs. Jones to get the PTA's official reaction on it?" suggested Susannah. "Jeff can go with you and get some shots." Jeff Perry was the main photographer, and the guy I thought would be good for Hailey.

I nodded and wrote this all on a list in my notebook.

Mr. Trigg interrupted. "Pardon me, but I think this article is too much work for one person to do in ten days." Part of his job as faculty advisor was to make sure our newspaper work didn't cut too much into our homework and sports time. "I think Ms. Martone needs a coreporter."

He looked around the group of twelve or so kids who were assembled in the newspaper office. "Mr. Lawrence. How about you?"

My stomach lurched and I looked behind me. Michael Lawrence had come in late and hadn't gotten a seat. He was leaning against the wall with his hands deep in the front pockets of his jeans. He never takes notes on anything because he has a famously photographic (and apparently DVR-like) memory. Just another reason why I worship him.

Michael nodded at Mr. Trigg, and Trigger said,

"Samantha, why don't you and Mr. Lawrence meet afterward and lay out your plan of attack. Equal work, equal time." I tried to nod casually but I thought I might faint. This was a dream come true and a nightmare all rolled into one! I looked down at my jeans and shirt and really wished I had borrowed a cute outfit from Allie this morning. And by "borrowed" I mean smuggled from her closet without her permission, because she would never give it.

Mr. Trigg had one more big announcement. "Now just a reminder to those of you who are returning to the *Cherry Valley Voice* and a notice to all of you who have just signed on. Facts are king in the newsroom. We print nothing but the truth, in black and white. Any quotation, any fact, must be substantiated. That means you need proof of everything you claim in your stories— every statistic, every quotation, everything! Does everyone understand?"

Duh! Facts are my life! I looked around and everyone was nodding. Of course! We all love facts. That's why we're here! Facts and writing, that is.

Susannah wrapped up the meeting and I gave Jeff Perry a few ideas for shots to get around school (the principal, Mr. Pfeiffer; Mrs. Jones, the head of the PTA; some teachers and kids). He left, and while the other kids milled around the room, I gathered my things and tried to think of something clever to say to Michael Lawrence when I met him at the door. But the next thing I knew he was tapping me on the shoulder.

"Hey, Pasty," he said. His voice is husky and kind of deep.

I could feel my face turn red and my shoulder almost burned where he had touched me. I stood up and turned around quickly, dropping my reporting notebook on the floor. Darn it! Why do I have to be so clumsy all the time?

"Hey, yourself," I said, bending over to pick up the notebook. I was trying to play it cool. The "Pasty" thing was embarrassing, and it was also starting to get a little annoying. I mean, it was eight years ago!

Michael was smiling at me. "Psyched to get the scoop?" he asked, tucking his hands under his armpits and rocking on his heels a little.

I didn't feel nervous as long as we were talking business. "Yeah. I think lots of people are pretty upset over these curriculum changes. I know, just for myself, it's hard to keep track of which class is which and what we're supposed to be doing there. I mean social studies is now called earth science."

Michael grew thoughtful. "I know. But I actually think in the long run it's going to be great for the school. Anyway, let's talk to at least two kids in every grade, the three parents, Mrs. Jones from the PTA, we'll also need three teachers, the principal, maybe an education expert or someone from the superintendent of schools . . ."

I had opened my notebook back up and was writing this all down. Michael looked at my notebook. "What are you doing?" he asked.

"Just getting it all down . . ." I said, writing.

"You mean you can't just remember?"

That was annoying. I looked up. "No. I can't. Not everyone has a fancy memory like you," I said.

"It's not about having a fancy memory," he said

patiently. "It's about being a good listener."

I glared at him. This was not going very well. "I *am* a good listener," I said. (*That's why I'm the Dear Know-It-All this year and you're not*, I wanted to scream, but I didn't.) "I just like having notes to refer back to. I like getting everything right, and I like having checklists."

He stared at me for an extra second. "Okay, Listy," he said finally. "Let's make a list of who does what."

Great! Another nickname! I groaned inwardly. But a huge grin had spread across his face and his eyes crinkled up at the outer corners into fans. At least he was cracking himself up. Two deep dimples appeared on either side of his smile, and I felt my breath catch in my throat at his cuteness. *Girl Sues Classmate for Harassment*, I thought. *Then Marries Him*, I added.

We divvied up the interviews and agreed to make an appointment to meet with the principal together, ideally during a lunch period, as soon as possible. Maybe we'll have time to sit together and go over things after our interview. But what if we run out of stuff to talk about? Or what if I have to eat spaghetti in front of him? Ugh. Messy!

As we wrapped up the details, Michael put his hand out. Seeing as how no one my age shakes hands, it took me a second to know what he was doing. I reached out my hand to shake his and felt myself melt into a puddle as his big, warm hand engulfed mine.

Michael left and I realized I needed to be at the soccer team tryouts ASAP. I smashed my notebook into my bag and headed toward the door.

"Samantha!" called Mr. Trigg, just as I was leaving. He came hurrying alongside me. "E-mail address, please. Stat," he said quietly, in a very calm tone. I knew it was so he could e-mail me the Know-It-All guidelines.

I pulled my notebook back out and quickly wrote it down for him, checking to make sure no one was looking before I ripped off the sheet and slyly palmed it to him. He kept his eyes on the room as he received it from me. I think he kind of enjoyed this spy stuff. I was starting to too.

"Excellent," he said. "Update TK. Cheerio!"

TK means "to come" in writing. It's a placeholder while you wait for more information. I knew what he meant and I nodded, feeling like a coconspirator. Then I headed off to report on the soccer tryouts.

As I trudged out to the school fields, my head spun with new assignments. Besides the big curriculum article and the soccer team tryouts, I had Know-It-All coming up and all of my schoolwork. I felt a jangly sense of nervous excitement about working with Michael Lawrence on the curriculum article. He was so smart, which made me think I might even learn something from him, but he was so cute it was distracting! I just hoped I didn't make a fool of myself.

"Samm-*my*!" Hailey called out from the far side of the field. The place was mobbed. Cherry Valley Middle School has three girls' and three boys' soccer teams: varsity, junior varsity, and recreational, which is for enthusiastic klutzes like me. I waded through crowds of seventh- and eighth-grade veterans, as well as sixth-grade hopefuls who were trying to look cool and not necessarily succeeding.

"Hey!" I said as I reached Hailey. "This place is a zoo."

"Why aren't you changed?" she asked.

I sighed loudly. "This is what I wear when I'm reporting," I said, gesturing to my jeans and my Toms shoes and the vintage leather messenger bag that I always wear slung diagonally across my back. I shrugged.

"Tsk, tsk," said Hailey. "You'll never know until you try."

"It's not like we'd even be on the same team, Hails." Varsity had been doing preseason for the past week. I'd be lucky to make the rec team.

But I did feel a little wistful as I surveyed the chatty group milling around outdoors on this sunny Indian summer afternoon. The teams looked like fun, so part of me really did want to participate. But I'm so clumsy and I have so much other stuff on my plate. And honestly, I really like to work alone.

I pulled out my notebook and began to do some man-on-the-streets, chatting with some kids I knew, some I didn't, asking for age, name, grade, and why they were trying out. Kids had lots of different reasons—for fun, for exercise, to get in shape, to prove to my dad I can make it (that one was a little sad), to impress a guy. Hmm. That one gave me pause.

Michael Lawrence is a major jock. Not a rock head, but just a very good athlete. One of those guys who never seems to stress out during a game. Not that I've watched him. Or, okay, not that many games. Only a few.

Now I wondered in panic if he even liked girls who were not athletic. Maybe indoorsy girls just don't cut it for him! Because, while he clearly enjoyed writing and was good at it, he didn't spend much time on it. The paper was more of a hobby for him, whereas football (quarterback) and baseball (pitcher) were his life. They were what he was known for around school.

I continued to wander around, getting good quotes ("Sometimes I imagine I'm in the World Cup and it makes me try harder," and "I picture a lion chasing me. It makes me run faster.") and chatting here and there as I made my way over to the coaches and captains for some good background material.

Hailey was with them now. As cocaptain, she would probably have some say over who made varsity. That was pretty powerful. She was stretching her shapely, tan legs and laughing with the coach. She even chucked him playfully on the shoulder with her fist. It looked like she was having fun. As I approached, the football team began their warm-up run right past the soccer field. All the soccer kids kind of stopped what they were doing and watched, because the football players had been training for all of August, and they were the acknowledged athletic kings of the school. I looked closely and spotted Michael, number fifteen and third in line. I watched him as he ran. He was so graceful and strong and tall. He just knew how to move.

As they passed the coaches, everyone called greetings back and forth. I heard Hailey yell something and she reached her hand out to Michael. He high-fived her as he ran by, and I felt a twinge of jealousy. Athletes were so easy and comfortable with one another, always laughing and joking and slapping one another on the butt and stuff. I did sort of wish I could be like that.

I resumed walking toward Hailey while, of course, still looking at Michael running by. It wasn't until I was halfway to the ground that I realized I'd tripped over a huge pile of cones. I landed on my hands and pushed myself back up pretty quickly, but I knew Michael had seen. He was turned back toward me and pumped his fist in the air. I thought I heard him yell, "Way to go, Pasty!" My face burned a hot, deep red.

Aargh!

"Sammy! Oh my gosh! Are you okay?!" Hailey was at my side in a flash but she was laughing. "That was classic! Did you do that on purpose?"

"What do you think?" I asked, annoyed. ***Girl Wipes Out in Front of Crush***. As if I'd do something that dumb on purpose. "And Michael saw me."

Hailey giggled. "I know. He laughed too."

"Great," I said.

"Well, it *looked* like you were doing it on purpose," said Hailey, not laughing anymore.

I sighed and made sure I had all my gear stowed in its proper place. Hailey picked up my notebook and handed it to me. It had flipped open to the page where I had written "Dear Know-It-All, by Samantha Martone" and then crossed it out.

"What's this?" she asked, looking curiously at the scribbles. She looked at me.

I grabbed the notebook. "Nothing." Great, that's all I needed. To blow my crush and my top secret job assignment all in one klutzy move.

Hailey was eyeing me carefully, though. After a brief silence she seemed to decide to lighten things up. "Practicing your signature, Mrs. Michael Lawrence?" she teased.

I nodded. "Yup." Great, now I was telling lies to my best friend too.

I decided I'd had enough of soccer tryouts for the day. "I'm hitting the road," I said.

"You don't want to stay and watch me shine? I'm way better out here than in language farts!" Hailey laughed at her own little joke.

"Taking a pass. I'll come back tomorrow and interview the coaches. Have fun."

Hailey looked like she wanted to say something more but the coach blew the whistle. She took one last look at me, then something caught her eye over my shoulder. I turned to see what she was looking at. It was the football team heading off through the woods trail. I looked back at Hailey and she looked at me. Then she saluted me and walked away.

I was left feeling lonely again, and this was *not* a feeling I liked.

Chapter 4

BUDDYBOOK: NOW MORE ADDICTIVE THAN EVER!

Mr. Trigg e-mailed me that night with the guidelines for Dear Know-It-All. They were pretty straightforward:

Do not reveal who you are. (*Yeah, we went over that already. Sheesh.*)

Do not reach out to the letter writer directly.

If someone seems to be in danger in any way, notify Mr. Trigg immediately. (*Danger?!? What kind of danger?*)

Keep it wholesome.

Be supportive and sympathetic. (*Hmm. Not my strong suit.*)

Keep it relevant. Broad subjects are better than very specific ones.

When in doubt, talk to Mr. Trigg.

All replies must be vetted by Mr. Trigg.

Don't forget, make it jazzy and readable!

Part of me wondered why Mr. Trigg didn't just write the column himself. It seemed like it would be easier. He probably had a lot more life experience and could actually give someone advice, whereas I have none! And honestly, I'm not good at being warm and fuzzy. I like facts and current events, not sob stories.

At the end of his e-mail, Mr. Trigg said that a few letters and e-mails had started to trickle in and that he would print them all and put them in a packet for me to pick up in the newsroom tomorrow. My mind began to whirl with possible intrigue and drama. What would these letters contain and how would I answer them? Me, the lovelorn klutz of the century. I hoped they'd all be about academics and extracurriculars so I could focus on the facts. I clearly had no idea what to tell anyone about dating or crushes or anything like that. Except don't trip on a pile of cones.

As I was sitting at my desk, reading his e-mail, Allie appeared in my doorway. I quickly minimized the e-mail window, kicking myself for not having created a password-protected folder yet to store the Know-It-All stuff. I couldn't risk someone coming over and going online on my computer, only to have her find the Know-It-All information! And I knew Allie sometimes poked around when she was bored.

"Hey," said Allie. She narrowed her eyes suspiciously at me. "What were you working on?"

"Oh, nothing. Just typing up quotes for my article on the curriculum changes."

Allie looked like she didn't really believe me, but she could hardly dive across my desk to prove me wrong. Instead she said, "Oh yeah. I heard something about that. They changed all the classes and now you're just taking, like, basket-weaving and folksinging or something?"

"Not exactly. It's just that instead of having regular subjects like math and English, they're integrating subjects so we study the same topics and themes but from different angles. It's called 'multidisciplinary.'"

Allie raised her eyebrows. "Fancy. But I still have no idea what you're talking about." She crossed her arms and leaned against the doorjamb.

I had to struggle to explain it myself. I could only do it by using examples. "Like, say we're studying the founding of the United States this year; in language arts we'll read books about the settlers and write diaries as if we're settlers. Then in earth science we'd talk about the New World's climate and geography and the crops they grew back then."

Allie looked begrudgingly impressed. "That's kind of cool. So it all ties in?"

"Yeah. It's just hard to keep track of what class you're in and what is expected of you. Like in earth science, am I supposed to be focusing on memorizing facts or creative writing? It takes a while to get used to."

"Huh. Well, I came to see if you have any printer paper I can have, please." Allie was clearly done with the topic.

"Yeah." I went under my desk and grabbed a

bunch of pages and handed them to her.

"Any word on who the Know-It-All is this year?" Allie asked suddenly.

I felt a jolt go through my body. Was the girl psychic or what? But I played it totally cool. "No. I haven't heard anything. Have you?"

"Why would I hear anything? High schoolers don't talk about middle schoolers. Ever," Allie said in a huff.

Right, so why are you wondering, I wanted to ask. But instead I said, "Oh. Well let me know if you accidentally hear anything." I thought that was good, throwing that in there.

"As if," said Allie, and she left.

Phew! That was a close call! Quickly, I created a desktop file and password-locked it (ML15 was the password, get it? Michael Lawrence, number fifteen), then I dropped the Trigg e-mail into it and relaxed back into my desk chair. I knew I should get started on my homework, but I decided I'd let myself have just a few minutes online first.

I trolled around *CNN* and the *Huffington Post* to see if there was any breaking news since I last checked an hour ago, but there really wasn't. I stopped by some of the celeb-watching sites and checked to see if there were any of my favorite postings—disgusting-celebrities-in-bathing-suits photos—but there weren't. I know those are totally mean and usually fake, but I can't help myself. Finally, I checked my in-box to see if I'd received any more e-mail, and there was one. It was yet another invitation to join Hailey on Buddybook.

I have to say now that I don't really get those sites where everyone posts all their updates. I know they make it easy for everyone to stay in touch with their friends from camp and whatnot, but I think they are boring and bogus and a waste of time. I mean, kids post stuff like, "I'm eating French fries." I mean, how unnewsy—not to mention dumb—is that? Do I really care? Does anyone else? I just don't get it. It just plain old wastes my time.

I deleted Hailey's invitation, fully knowing that she would e-mail it to me again, and then I quit my e-mail and Internet connection. Next I signed off the Internet for an hour. This is what I have to do in order to get any work done. Otherwise

I will continue to check, check, check the news all the time. Mom taught me how to do it after I started taking waaaay too long last year to finish my homework. She made me keep track of what I was doing when, and she added up that I spent way more time on the Internet than on math. Whoops!

Sure enough, not one minute later, my phone rings and it's Hailey.

"Are you ignoring my buddy request?" she asks, without even saying hi.

I sighed heavily. "Hailey. You know how I feel about those sites. It's just a waste of time. It's fake information. It's information clutter. Plus, I'm in touch with everyone I want to be in touch with."

"But it's so fun. If you sign up, we can play cards together and join fan groups together and I can post funny photos and links for things I find online . . ."

"Yeah, but you can e-mail me all that stuff too," I said. "And we can play games in person!"

"Well . . . maybe you'll join when you see the photos from football practice that Jeff Perry put up today."

Football practice? Hmm.

"Why? Are they funny?" I asked. "Is there one of Michael?"

But of course, Hailey wouldn't say. "You'll just have to join! Ta-ta!" And she hung up.

I looked at my phone and then I sighed heavily. That was an annoying conversation. I am not joining Buddybook. Just on principle alone, I don't want to do it. Time wasting, fake-informational, nonfactual, uncensored, unedited, free-for-all, invasion of privacy . . .

But the football photos? Those I had to see.

I began the incredibly difficult and boring process of unlocking my Time Out application. Mom made it really hard so that I couldn't just click back on it. Fifteen minutes later I was logged on to Buddybook and climbing all over that site. I was like a sugar addict who'd been let loose in a candy store.

I had accepted Hailey's request, which lead me to all of our friends' pages, but I froze when I saw Michael Lawrence's name as a buddy up on her wall. If I visited his page, would he know I'd been there? Would he be able to tell? Would it somehow send him a buddy request from me? And what if he didn't accept?! I was too scared to find out the hard way so I didn't click on it.

Instead, I looked at Jeff Perry's page and scrolled through all the football photos he'd uploaded. There were some really hideous-but-funny ones of guys straining through warm-ups, making ugly faces and stuff. Some were so bad I had to wonder if they'd mind that Jeff put them up there. There was one of this kid Andy Ryan where his belly was hanging over the top of his pants. It was kind of a bad angle, but he's also pretty chubby and it was just not flattering.

Maybe boys just don't care that much about how they look in photos, I thought. But I would. Especially ones online for the entire world to see.

I scrolled down a little farther and stopped dead in my tracks. There was a close-up of Michael Lawrence, his hair sweaty, his arm drawn back to throw the football, and his face all serious and concentrated. His tan made his blue eyes look even bluer, and his mouth was open, and he looked so, so gorgeous. Like a movie star! It took my breath away. I wondered if there was a way I could pull a copy off Jeff's page and make this photo my desktop background!

"Wow! Lookin' good!"

I jumped ten feet in the air. "Allie! You scared me!" I hadn't heard her coming this time.

"Sorry!" she said, laughing.

"There's such a thing as privacy, you know!"

"Not on Buddybook, there's not!" Allie laughed again. "Welcome to the dark side, little Miss 'I'm Never Joining That Time-Waster Site'! Does Mom know you joined?"

"No. Do I need her permission?" I said. I was offended by her condescending tone.

Allie shrugged. "I did."

"Oh whatever," I said. "I might not even stay a member. I just wanted to see these photos."

Suddenly my in-box pinged. "Finally! Welcome aboard!" the message read. It was from Hailey, of course.

Allie laughed. "You're going to be addicted in no time," she said. "It happens to everyone. Even the best of us."

Humph. Not me. I can shut it off anytime. "It's so not up my alley," I said, clicking the window shut.

"Right," said Allie.

"Why do you keep popping in here anyway and invading my privacy?"

"Oh. Could I please have some paper clips?"

I groaned and doled some out. "You should have come to Staples with me and Mom when she asked you to last week."

"I was busy." Allie shrugged. "Anyway, I knew you'd get plenty. Mom too. Thanks!"

As soon as she left, I was back on Buddybook, looking for more photos of Michael. Before I knew it, an entire hour had passed. If Mom ever heard about this, she'd install something to send me into lockdown forever! I quickly disabled my account and quit out every aspect of Buddybook. I knew I'd been right before! It wasn't for me. I need to stick to facts and useful uses of my time.

Well, now that I knew how addictive yet boring Buddybook was, I could make an accurate argument against it. Just like in journalism: present the facts, let people draw their own opinions.

The only good thing to come out of all this computer time was that I now knew I needed to rearrange my room so I that my back wasn't facing the door when I was at my desk. I was tired of people sneaking up on me and I was tired of having my privacy invaded.

I disabled my Internet again and got started on the Supreme Court case I had to argue next week in front of my humanities class, whatever that was.

Chapter 5

MARTONE THROWS IN THE TOWEL

I kept sneaking peeks at Michael Lawrence the next morning in homeroom. I couldn't believe the photo I'd seen of him the night before. He was just so gorgeous. Finally, he caught me staring.

"What?" he asked.

I was embarrassed. "Oh, um. Nothing. Just . . . did you get any good quotes yet for the article?"

"Sam Martone, ace reporter. Are you always working?" asked Michael.

I shrugged. "Aren't you?" Always good to answer a question with a question, I say.

"Except when I'm on Buddybook," he said with a grin. Then he turned his back on me because our teacher was taking attendance.

What?! My face flamed. Did he know I'd joined? Oh my gosh, did he know I had been looking at pictures of him? What if Jeff Perry could tell I'd viewed his photos and told Michael? What if they could tell how long I'd lingered over that one hottie photo of Michael? Oh my gosh. I hated Buddybook now more than ever! It was a total invasion of privacy! It was worse than Allie!

I turned to my right and glared at Hailey. She looked back at me innocently. "What?" she mouthed. I sighed loudly and shook my head. She'd gotten me into this whole thing, but it actually wasn't her fault. It wasn't like she'd gone ahead and signed me up for Buddybook without my knowing. I only had myself to blame.

I felt something scratch my arm and I looked to my left again. Fred Ogden was passing me a note, and he jerked his head to indicate it was from Michael Lawrence, who wasn't even looking at me. Oh great. What now? Quickly I grabbed the note and held it flat on my desk under my hand. I waited to make sure the teacher hadn't seen. Then I casually smoothed it open and read: *Fourth period lunch tomorrow. Mr. Pfeiffer interview. His office.*

I flipped the note over. There was nothing else. Great. My huge crush finally passes me a note and it's all business. ***Martone Throws in the Towel,*** I thought dejectedly. This day could only get better.

Fine, I wrote, then I quickly passed it to Fred when the teacher wasn't looking. Two could play at this game.

During study hall, I went to the newspaper office. One of the many cool things about working on the paper is that you get to spend your free periods and study halls in the office if you want to. It's a privilege. Obviously if your grades drop, you lose the privilege, but it's pretty cool to have a place to go and kind of lounge or get work done or chat with friends.

As I entered the office, Mr. Trigg called out, "Samantha! Hello! I've left the curriculum materials for you in your mailbox!"

All of the staff reporters and editors and art/layout people have their own mailboxes in the *Voice* office. I turned to mine and spied a manila envelope, which I grabbed and stuffed into my messenger bag. It had to be the Dear Know-It-All letters in there.

"Thanks, Mr. Trigg," I called.

He nodded vigorously and tried to look very, very busy, so I knew for sure it was letters. I was excited! I couldn't wait to demonstrate my new and improved snappy writing skills in this hot column! It was really happening, now!

If only I could rip the envelope open right here and read the entire contents right now, I thought. But obviously that would be a bad idea.

"Yo," said Jeff Perry, walking in the door behind me. "Saw you joined Buddybook last night."

"Ugh!" I said. "I hate that thing! I already quit!"

Jeff laughed. "That's what they all say the first time. You'll be back!" Jeff was still pretty small for his age, but he was wiry and a good athlete. Fast. His head was tiny, but he had enormous eyes and lots of wild, curly black hair. It was like his features were waiting for his body to grow into them. He's pretty hyper too, like he has the energy to run a much bigger body so there's a lot to spare. Maybe he'll slow down one day when he grows. "Did you like my football photos?" he asked. "Some of them were pretty hilarious!" He laughed.

I made a face. "I don't know, Jeff. Don't you

think some of those guys will be mad at you for putting their photos up there like that? Some of them aren't so great."

"Nah." Jeff waved a hand dismissively. "Guys don't care about stuff like that."

Just then the door banged open. It was Michael! "Hey, Pasty," he said to me. "Yo, Perry, get those photos of me off Buddybook. Now."

"Dude! Come on! They're great! What do you care?" asked Jeff.

"I care because you do not have my permission to put photos of me on Buddybook, that's why." Michael went over to his mailbox to see if he had anything in there.

"No one else cares," Jeff called after him.

"I don't care about other people," said Michael, doubling back. "And anyway, you're wrong. I bet all those guys tell you to get their photos down today. Especially Andy."

Huh. Maybe boys do care how they look in photos after all.

"Whatever," said Jeff. "But you look good in yours. Doesn't he, Sam?"

Girl Dies of Embarrassment in Newspaper Office.

"What? Oh. Wait . . ." My brain was scrambling as I tried to play it cool. "Which photos?"

Michael was looking at me closely.

Jeff sighed in aggravation. "You know, the football ones? The ones where you said everyone looked bad and was going to be mad at me?"

I couldn't look at Michael at all now. "I didn't say *everyone* looked bad!" Oh my gosh. This was not going well. I snuck a peek at Michael. His face was red now too! I could hardly say Michael looked hot and everyone else looked terrible!

"Whatever. This is stupid. Just take 'em down, Perry!" Michael snarled, and he left the office, the door banging shut behind him.

Um. Yikes.

"Thanks a lot, Martone," said Jeff, shaking his head. He collapsed into the office sofa and laid his head back, closing his eyes. "Way to back me up."

"You never should have put them up," I said, and I left the office too. Should I have told Michael he looked good in the photos and not to worry?

Would it seem like I liked him if I did that? Maybe I insulted him without meaning to. And now Jeff was mad at me too. This day stinks!

Maybe the Know-It-All letters would be great and it would cheer me up. I was dying to read through them but where could I go to get some privacy?

Duh!

I strode down the hall to the girls' bathroom and pushed open the door. Phew. Empty.

Inside a stall, I locked the door and put the lid down on the toilet, then I sat and opened the envelope. There actually were curriculum materials from Mr. Trigg, but there were also three letters in envelopes that had been slit open. Mr. Trigg reads them all first to make sure they're not hostile letters to the editor disguised as Know-It-All letters, not that that ever actually happens.

The first one was on pink stationery with a matching pink envelope. Obviously from a girl. Or maybe from someone who wanted us to *think* it was from a girl, I suddenly thought. Hmmm. My journalist antenna tingled as I began to read.

Dear Know-It-All,

I still sleep with a teddy bear named Pal every night. This is kind of embarrassing because I am now in the eighth grade. I don't want anyone to know, but when I have sleepovers I can't get to sleep without him. What should I do?

From,
Sleepless without Pal

Ha! That was a funny one! Time to grow up, I'd say. Lose the Pal. I wondered if a boy had stolen his sister's stationery to write the note and throw us off his trail. It was possible. I felt proud of myself for being such a good investigator to even think of such a thing. I set it aside. It could be good for later in the year if I didn't have anything better, but it was kind of lame for the launch of this year's column. I wanted something juicier.

Next!

This one was handwritten on white computer paper in a business envelope. As I read, I saw lots of misspellings and grammatical errors that made me wince. Do I even go to the same school as this person? I wondered.

Dear Know-It-All,

You know how somtimes things are sucking at home and you, like, dont want to be there at all ever? Where should you go, like, insted?

Thanks.

From,
A guy

Okay. Wow. That was kind of heavy for the first Dear Know-It-All of the year. Don't know how to help that guy! I bit my lower lip and moved it to the bottom of the pile.

The last letter had been done on a computer. It said:

Hey Mr. Know-It-All,

What do you do when you and your best friend have a crush on the same person?

Signed,
Unlucky Taste

Whoa! That was a juicy one! I couldn't even imagine what would happen in that situation. The poor guy. He should just tell his friend and then he and the friend can duke it out over the girl, I would say!

This would make a great, very jazzy first column of the year, I decided. I'd wait to see if anything else came in, but I felt secure at having at least one great option. Not that I had a clue what to say to this person, but I'd deal with that later. (Maybe I could research it online somehow.)

I folded the letter up and stuffed it back in its envelope, then I put all three letters back in the manila envelope from Mr. Trigg, tightening the bolt on the back and wedging it all back down into my messenger bag. There had to be a safer way to transport these letters. What if my bag fell into the wrong hands?

I exited the stall, washed my hands, and went to meet Hailey. Hopefully lunch with my BFF would cheer me up!

Chapter 6

MARTONE FIRES BEST FRIEND, BECOMES HERMIT

★ ★ ★

Lunch was gross. I sat with Hailey and picked at my chimichanga and JELL-O.

"Mr. Pfeiffer should have revamped the lunch menu before he took on the curriculum," said Hailey.

"Oooh!" I whipped out my notebook. "Can I quote you? That would be good for my article," I said, copying down Hailey's words.

"Sure. Whatever. I'm full of juicy quotes," she said. "Oh look. Here comes lover boy!"

I looked up and there was Michael with his lunch tray, looking for a place to sit.

"Yoo-hoo! Number fifteen!" called Hailey.

"Hailey! No!" I hissed, but it was too late.

"Why not?" she said, turning to me.

I sighed. "Just . . ."

"Hey, Hailey. Hey, Pasty," said Michael.

"Want to join us?" asked Hailey.

"Okay. Just for a minute, because I'm actually sitting with Walter once he finishes clearing out the buffet line."

Hailey sat up straight and fluffed her hair with her hands, leaving her dangly earrings jangling all over the place. This fluffing thing was an annoying new habit she had, I'd noticed.

"Quite the photo of you on Buddybook last night," she said to Michael in kind of a flirty way.

Oh great, here we go again. Can't anyone talk about anything but Buddybook?

Michael did not look happy. "Sam here thinks it's terrible." He gestured to me with a jut of his chin.

"*What?* I do not!" I sputtered. "That is totally inaccurate!"

Michael shrugged and looked away. "I believe the quote was 'I didn't say everyone looked bad,'" He made little quotation marks in the air.

"That's not what I said!" I protested.

Michael tapped his temple. "Fancy memory, remember?"

I crossed my arms over my chest and huffed. "Well, that's not what I meant." Did I dare to tell him he looked gorgeous in the photo? My body surged with adrenaline at the idea of being that bold. Could I do it?

"Well, I thought you looked gorgeous in the photo," said Hailey.

Wait, *what*?

Did she just say exactly what I was thinking?

I looked at Hailey. Then I looked at Michael. He had ducked his head shyly, a move I'd never seen him make before. Michael Lawrence? Shy? My eyes widened. I couldn't process this.

"Yeah," said Michael dismissively, as if he was saying, "No."

"It's true, right, Sammy?" Hailey nudged me.

"Hailey!" Was she trying to mortify me or what?

"Tell him how good he looked!" she teased.

Oh my goodness. I wanted to die. I covered my face with my hands. This was so embarrassing.

"There's Walter. I've gotta go," said Michael.

And he stood up with his tray and hurried away.

"Sam!" Hailey hit me on the arm. "What is your problem?"

"What is yours?" I said. I was furious. "Why are you trying to rat me out? Why do you want Michael Lawrence to know I'm in love with him?"

"That's not what I was trying to say! Couldn't you tell how embarrassed he was? I was trying to make him feel better. It *is* a great photo of him. Just acknowledging that doesn't declare your love for him!"

"Yes it does!"

"Oh, please. He's just a person too, you know. It wouldn't kill you to be nice to him."

"What are you talking about? I'm always nice to him!"

Hailey shrugged and rolled her eyes. "Not really."

"What?! Yes I am!"

"Sam, you hardly even talk to him unless it's necessary. I bet you don't know anything about him."

"Why, do you?"

Hailey shrugged again. "Yeah." She looked down at her fingernails.

"Like what?" I asked.

"I don't know."

"Okay, so, then . . ."

She counted things off on her fingers. "Well, I know that his favorite lunch is cheeseburgers and his favorite class is language farts, and I know that he throws lefty and he has had two concussions and if he gets another he can't play football anymore. And I know that—"

"Wait. Stop. Hold it!" I said, putting my palm flat out like a traffic cop. "How do you know all this?"

Hailey shrugged again. "I don't know. I just talk to him, like a normal person. I ask him questions and then I listen to the answers. It's not so hard. It's called being a friend."

I tossed my head. "Well, I'm not his *friend*."

"Okay. Whatever then," said Hailey.

"It's a little annoying that you're suddenly the expert on Michael Lawrence," I said quietly.

Hailey was looking off at the other side of the

cafeteria. I followed her gaze and saw Walter and Michael. They were laughing and joking around like they didn't have a care in the world.

"At least I didn't hurt his feelings," Hailey said back, without looking at me.

"Oh come on, boys don't have feelings!" I said.

Hailey looked at me like she was shocked. Then she rolled her eyes and laughed. "You are hopeless," she said.

"Wait, do they?" I asked.

Hailey laughed harder. *"Really* hopeless!" She stood up and collected her stuff and her tray. "Come on. Let's go."

Martone Fires "Best Friend." Becomes Hermit, I thought.

Chapter 7

MARTONE BACK FROM BRINK OF DISASTER

Seventh period came too soon. I was so nervous about our meeting that for the first time in years I was actually dreading seeing Michael Lawrence. I dragged my feet all the way down to Mr. Pfeiffer's office for our interview, nearly making myself late. Michael was standing in the hall outside, tapping his foot impatiently.

"Come on!" he hissed. "We can't be late!"

"Sorry," I whispered. "We're not, anyway."

We checked in with Mr. Pfeiffer's secretary and she told us to have a seat in the waiting area. I busied myself getting my pen and notebook out, and when Michael saw what I was doing he rolled his eyes and looked away.

"What?" I asked in a quiet voice.

He shrugged. "I just think it's more respectful to listen carefully," he said.

"Well that may be, but how are we going to be sure we get the quotes right?" I asked.

He tapped the side of his head again.

I wasn't buying it. "But your fancy memory isn't written out as proof, in case for some unbelievable and rare reason, you get a word wrong. We can't misquote the principal!" Michael had a lot of nerve.

"We won't," he said definitively.

"You know what? Fine. Have it your way." I snapped my notebook shut and stowed it and my pen back in my bag. I wished I had a tape recorder, but if he wanted to do it this way, then it was his responsibility.

"Okay, kids, he can see you now. Go on in," said the secretary.

We stood up and crossed to the door to the office. Mr. Pfeiffer was on the phone and smiled and waved us in. It was an awkward moment. Michael gestured for me to go first through the door, but then I wasn't sure if I should stand in the doorway or head right in and sit down. I started to go in, then changed my mind and backed out again, right into Michael. He must have been just shutting the door, and it was crazy chaos but somehow the door shut on his hand. Hard.

"Ow!" he shouted.

I whipped around to see what was happening, and Michael was clutching his left hand and biting down hard on his lip.

"What?"

"Ow. My fingers. Ow." His eyes were closed and for a horrible moment I wondered if he might actually cry. (Do boys cry? I mean big boys? I have no idea!)

Mr. Pfeiffer had hung up the phone and was at Michael's side in a flash.

"Michael, I saw that whole thing happen. Oh gosh. I'm so sorry." Mr. Pfeiffer ducked his head out of the office and called to his secretary. "Mary, can you get us some ice from the nurse, please? Michael Lawrence just had his hand slammed in the door!"

"Uh-oh! Right away!" she called back.

"Michael, why don't you sit down . . ." Mr. Pfeiffer

reached and pulled one of his guest chairs toward Michael. Michael sat down heavily.

I didn't know what to do.

"Can you move it?" Mr. Pfeiffer asked.

"I don't know . . ." muttered Michael, his jaw clenched tightly.

It seemed like an eternity but finally the door opened and the nurse was there. "Hi, honey. You poor thing. Let's take a look . . ."

Michael opened his eyes and looked up at her, and I could see that there actually were tears in his eyes! Oh my goodness! I took another step back and banged into a little side table, nearly knocking it over. I looked up in embarrassment but no one had seen. Phew.

"What happened, sweetie?" asked the nurse gently.

Michael could hardly speak through the pain. His voice came out in little gasps. "I was walking in behind her . . . and I had my hand on the door . . . to pull it closed. Then . . . she backed into me . . . and I didn't get my hand out in time."

Wait, me? It was my fault?

Mr. Pfeiffer was nodding in agreement.

Oh my goodness. My hand flew up to cover my mouth. "Michael, I'm . . . I didn't realize!"

They all looked up at me like I'd just appeared from Mars.

"Don't worry, honey. Accidents happen," said the nurse.

Accidents! But I didn't even think I'd done anything! I mean, he was the one who slammed the door.

The nurse called Michael's mom to see if it was okay to give him aspirin. Then she gave Michael two aspirin to take with some water. Next she brought a bucket of ice and told Michael to soak his hand in it for a while, and to come up and see her again afterward. "It's not broken, sweetie," she said. "But we might wrap it up in an ACE bandage just to be safe. It's not your throwing hand anyway, is it?" she asked.

But Michael nodded. That's right. Hailey had said he throws lefty. Darn it!

Michael was nodding. "Yep, I'm a lefty."

The nurse bit her lip. "Well, let's just see how it does with a little ice, okay?" She and Mr. Pfeiffer exchanged a look that seemed to say they'd discuss all this later, then she nodded, patted Michael on the back, and left.

"Okay, where were we?" said Michael with a little laugh.

I was still standing there in shock. "Michael, I'm so . . . I didn't mean to . . . I mean, I'm sure I didn't . . ." Should I apologize for something I didn't even think was my fault? Maybe it was my fault. But it was truly an accident.

Michael shook his head. "Don't worry about it. It was an accident."

Mr. Pfeiffer leaned back against the front of his desk. "We can reschedule the interview, kids. Just relax here for as long as you need and then I can move some stuff around on my calendar and get you back in here . . ."

"No, no, I'm fine," protested Michael. "Really. Now that the numbness is kicking in . . ." He winced.

I felt terrible. "I'm so sorry," I said finally. "I'm really, really sorry."

Michael looked up at me and smiled. "It's fine," he said. "Let's start the interview."

Mr. Pfeiffer looked at him carefully. "If you're sure . . ."

Michael nodded. "I'm sure."

The next twenty minutes were, without a doubt, the most interesting time I'd ever spent in school. Mr. Pfeiffer outlined how the new curriculum was designed to help students deal with the onslaught of information that grows every day from thousands of different directions. He talked about books, magazines, the Internet, TV news, social media, libraries, newspapers, blogs, Wikipedia, and how to evaluate the quality of your sources, how to incorporate what he called the quantifiable information (facts) with qualifiable information (opinions and feelings) to create what he called "the whole understanding."

At first I had a really hard time listening to Mr. Pfeiffer without writing everything down. I was also really nervously looking down at Michael's hand and hoping that I just *thought* it was swelling. It looked kind of puffy. But when I started to relax and really hear what Mr. Pfeiffer was saying, I found I was able to ask useful questions and have more of a conversation with him than an interview. It was actually fun!

Michael was into it too, and it felt cool to have a conversation with a grown-up where he wasn't talking down to us, but really explaining himself and making sure we understood. Plus, he was so enthusiastic, it was contagious.

"Our goal, in essence, is to have you leave here with the skills to be able to tell a great story," Mr. Pfeiffer said. "Because when you think about it, isn't that what everything comes down to in life? Telling a great story?"

"Wow," I said, nodding. "True."

"Very cool," agreed Michael.

"Are you going to come to the Parent Teacher Association meeting on Thursday?" Mr. Pfeiffer asked. "There should be some lively debate there that you might incorporate into your article."

I nodded hard. "Definitely!" I said.

"Good." He nodded happily. "Michael, how's the hand?"

Michael had it resting out of the ice on a pile of paper towels on his lap. "It's going to be okay, I think," he said.

"All right. Well, I've got to run to a meeting

with the superintendent of schools. And you know what? I'll see if he'd mind if one of you gives him a call to get a quote for your article, okay?"

"That would be great! Thanks!" I said, standing. "And thanks for your time and everything. It was really interesting."

Michael stood too. He looked around to see how he was going to carry everything.

"Here. I'll help you," I offered, reaching for his book bag.

"Stay back!" he said, half joking. "I don't need another injury."

I bit my lip. That was kind of mean. It's not like I had directly hurt him before.

So Mr. Pfeiffer lifted the ice bucket and Michael's backpack and helped us out through the door.

"Mary, will you get Mr. Lawrence an elevator pass, please?" he asked his secretary.

"Really, let me help," I said. I lifted Michael's backpack from Mr. Pfeiffer and hoisted it on my back. It was heavy. "Ready?" I asked.

Mary handed Michael the elevator pass, and we shook hands with Mr. Pfeiffer.

"Thanks again, Mr. Pfeiffer. You really made me see this in a whole new way," I said.

"Glad to help," said Mr. Pfeiffer. "See you kids soon! And I'll let you know what the superintendent says!"

We walked out into the hallway and I suddenly felt really awkward.

"I can carry my backpack," said Michael.

"Well, at least let me get you to the elevator," I said.

Michael shrugged. "Thanks. I don't want to take you out of your way."

"It's not out of my way. I've got to go up to science anyway and the stairs are right there." We were speaking like we were strangers. And suddenly I could see that in most ways, we were.

Michael looked down at his elevator pass. "I'm only going one floor up to the nurse's office. But it says I'm allowed to bring a friend on the elevator with me."

"Oh," I said, looking down at the elevator pass.

"But I'm not sure you're my friend," he said. "Friends don't try to maim each other."

My head snapped up in shock, but then I saw that he was smiling.

"I am your friend," I said. And I smiled back.

"Okay, then right this way. Good thing there's a wide door . . ." He gestured me onto the elevator.

"Very funny," I said.

I sighed as we climbed aboard. *Martone Back from the Brink of Disaster*, I thought.

"I didn't know you threw lefty . . ." I said as the doors closed.

My mom was waiting for me when I got home from school that afternoon.

"Samantha, Allie tells me you joined Buddybook without my permission," she said before I'd even put down my messenger bag.

"Well . . ." I was caught off guard. "I did, but I've already quit. Wait, when did she tell you?" Our mom had been at the gym when we'd left for school this morning, so we hadn't seen her.

"She texted me," said my mom.

"That is so annoying! Now she's texting to meddle in my life?"

My mom smiled a wry smile. "Isn't that what social

media is all about? Meddling in people's lives?"

"Yeah, it sure seems like it." We walked up the steps to the kitchen and I started making a big snack of melted cheddar cheese on Triscuits. I was still suffering the effects of not eating lunch.

"Listen, sweetheart, Buddybook is a big commitment. I don't want to see you wasting your time on it before we've had a chance to discuss our family's rules and guidelines for using it. If you decide you're going to do it again, you'll need my permission."

I waved my hand at her. "Don't worry. I'm over it," I said.

My mom looked at me for a long minute. Then she said, "Okay, but since I have your attention on the subject, there are just three things to always remember: One, only you can control your image online—written, video, photographic, all of it. And you need to be vigilant about it. Two, whatever goes online stays online forever. It never goes away. And three, never put anything online that it wouldn't be okay for everyone to see, including me, or your grandmother, or Dr. Sobel . . ."

Dr. Sobel is our dentist. "Mom!" I laughed.

She smiled. "Just so you get my point. *Anyone*."

I nodded and started eating my crackers. "Okay. I get it."

We were quiet for a minute and then she said, "How's the new curriculum?"

"Fine. Oh, that just made me remember . . ." I pulled the envelope out of my messenger bag and carefully took out the new curriculum materials. I didn't let my mom see the Know-It-All letters. I had my professional standard of anonymity to uphold, after all. Even if Mr. Trigg *had* told her, we didn't have to talk about it.

I laid the curriculum materials out on the table between us and we looked at them.

"It's interesting," said my mom. "I can see both sides."

"What *are* both sides?" I asked. A lot of this was still unclear to me.

"Well, the traditionalists like the subject-based approach, where in math you learn math and in English you learn reading and writing. But in the new curriculum you learn to look at topics from many angles. You learn how to sift through different kinds of information. You learn how to ask questions. It might not work for every kind of student."

"I already know how to ask questions," I said with a grin.

"You sure do, sweetheart," said my mom, rubbing my back briskly. "So you will do just fine. Just remember, not everything has a one-word answer. Not everything is cut-and-dried."

"I know, Mom. I tried to remember that when I was sitting in the principal's office this afternoon."

"WHAT?!" Her shocked reaction was just what I'd hoped for.

"Gotcha!" I laughed. "I interviewed him about the new curriculum."

"Oh, Samantha, you nearly gave me heart failure! Well, just remember to always be polite and be pleasant. My dear grandmother used to say . . ."

"I know, I know . . ."

"You catch more bees with honey!" We said it at the same time and laughed.

Chapter 8

STOMACH RUCKUS DRIVES AWAY HOTTIE

I was lying in bed that night, thinking back over the day and especially about the meeting with Mr. Pfeiffer, when suddenly, I sat bolt upright.

Oh my goodness! We'd been snowed!

The whole time that Michael and I had been meeting with Mr. Pfeiffer, the principal's enthusiasm swept us along and we'd never asked him any hard questions or anything! How had I, of all people, not asked any probing questions? How had I, of all people, gone though that whole half hour without trying to poke any holes in his story or his facts? Was it because I wasn't using my notebook? Yes. Was I distracted by Michael's presence? Yes. Was I distracted by the hand-slamming incident? Yes. Was

I intimidated by the principal? Yes, yes, yes, and yes!

Martone Blows First Major Interview!

I was ashamed of myself. I'd wasted an important opportunity and Mr. Trigg would have been very disappointed in me. It was not the behavior of an editor in chief in training! I was behaving like a rookie!

Now my adrenaline was pumping and I had to turn on the light and grab my notebook. I brainstormed some questions for Mr. Pfeiffer and wrote them down, vowing to myself that I would ask them at the PTA meeting. I could not let another opportunity escape me.

Once I had everything safely logged in my notebook, I began to calm down. Reviewing my new set of questions, my heart stopped racing and I began to feel like I was back in control. I turned off my light and lay there in the darkness, resolving to be tougher than ever in my reporting. *Facts matter*, I scolded myself. *Don't be distracted by your emotions*, I chanted in my head.

As much as I love news reporting, I still have a long way to go.

The PTA meeting in the school auditorium on Thursday night was mobbed. Nearly everyone who was there was ready to debate for and against the new curriculum. It could get rowdy. Actually, I hoped it would! That would make a great story.

I got there early and snagged a seat in the second row near the center. I put my messenger bag on the chair next to me. Michael had said if I got there first, I should save him a seat, but I hadn't seen any sign of him. I knew he had football practice, but it didn't usually run late. Meanwhile, I wished I'd had a chance to get a snack between study hall and visiting the final day of soccer tryouts for my story on that. I was starving.

The room filled quickly. I didn't realize this was going to be such a hot event! About twenty people asked if someone was sitting in the seat next to me and after I'd said yes enough times, I started getting a little annoyed with Michael. If he didn't come, I would look like a liar.

Finally at 6:01, Mrs. Jones, the parent head of the PTA, called the meeting to order. She and Mr. Pfeiffer and the dean of students and the assistant principal were all sitting at a table up on the stage. They did a bunch of meeting-ish stuff, like making announcements, and then Mrs. Jones said they would welcome any commentary on the curriculum changes so far. I didn't want to lead with my questions so I sat back and bided my time, taking notes.

The first person to stand was a sixth-grade parent. She read from a prepared statement that said American education is about learning the basics in common with everyone else in the country. To take a new approach was un-American. A bunch of people clapped. Mr. Pfeiffer listened thoughtfully, but he didn't say anything.

Next Mrs. Perry stood up. Jeff was at the event taking photos for the *Voice* and I looked at him to see if he was happy or embarrassed that his mom was talking. It looked like he was pretending he didn't know her, but he did snap her photo.

"Our children spend enough time on the Internet," she said angrily. "We are not paying huge school taxes to have our children sit on computers all day. They can do that at home!"

Mrs. Perry sat down in a huff.

A bunch of people clapped and now Jeff's face was red. Looks like Mrs. Perry is a little sick of Jeff's Buddybook obsession.

Just then there was a little activity at the end of my row and I turned to see Michael sidling in, apologizing. A smile bloomed on my face and I tried to force it away. This was business after all and he was late.

"Hey," he whispered.

"Hey," I whispered back, trying to collect myself now that he was sitting so close I could feel the warmth radiating off his arms. He had obviously come straight from football practice, since his hair was wet and he smelled all soapy. All of my annoyance melted away.

"Did I miss anything?" he asked.

"Only Perry's mom freaking out about Buddybook in the classrooms," I whispered.

"Seriously?" he said, turning to face me.

"Nah." I shook my head and smiled, and he swatted my knee with a flyer he had in his hand.

"You should've been there yesterday when

Andy Ryan threatened to beat the tar out of Perry if he didn't take down his photo," whispered Michael.

Some lady shushed us, and Michael turned to listen to the meeting.

Mr. Pfeiffer was still answering Mrs. Perry, saying that schools need to educate kids how to sift through all the junk out there, and part of that is using the Internet, and that our school is educating kids for the future, not just the present. "Though computers will in no way replace books or teachers at Cherry Valley Middle School," he added. I wrote that down as a quote.

Mrs. Perry looked skeptical but didn't say anything more.

Meanwhile, my stomach knew it was my usual dinnertime. I only hoped it wouldn't growl audibly, with Michael sitting right next to me. Holy embarrassing! *Stomach Ruckus Drives Away Hottie, Girl Dies of Embarrassment.*

An eighth grader's father stood up to ask how the school was planning on handling reading levels now that even science and math would incorporate reading. "With some kids very proficient, and others at a more remedial level, how will you handle such a reading-driven curriculum?" he asked. That was a great question, I thought, thinking of Hailey and writing it down.

Oops. I could feel a stomach growl coming. I bent to look for gum in my bag and ended up accidentally tossing my notebook on the floor. It made a loud rustling slam as it hit the floor, and a bunch of people turned to look—Michael among them. He reached to pick it up for me, and my face burned as I took it from him. Great. Another strike against my notebook—it was noisy and sloppy and always subject to my klutziness. And after all that I didn't have any gum to hold off my hunger pangs!

Worse, I had missed Mr. Pfeiffer's reply about reading levels.

"Did you get that?" I whispered to Michael.

He nodded.

"Good."

There was a lull in the questioning so I flipped my notebook open and decided it was now or never. I had to rectify our snoozing through the interview with Mr. Pfeiffer the other day and, I had to admit, I also wanted to impress Michael.

"Mr. Pfeiffer." I was on my feet and talking before I'd even had a chance to get nervous about it.

"Yes, Samantha," said Mr. Pfeiffer with a smile. He obviously figured this would be an easy question from a friendly person on his team. Ha!

"Mr. Pfeiffer, who made the decision to change the curriculum and what are you doing to train the teachers in the new curriculum?"

I didn't think I was being harsh. Mr. Pfeiffer had been nice to us in his office and about Michael's hand and everything, but news is news.

Mr. Pfeiffer's smile faded. "That is a very good question, Samantha. Ahem." Mr. Pfeiffer cleared his throat. It seemed like he was stalling for time. "The decision was reached in agreement with the superintendent of schools and the board of education."

"On behalf of our school who made the decision?"

"It was . . . just me. I did." Mr. Pfeiffer looked uncomfortable.

Ooh! This was news! Now I was getting somewhere!

"So you volunteered for us to be guinea pigs, without input from anyone else on staff?"

A lot of the parents clapped and a couple of people shouted, "Bravo!" I tried not to listen to them. This wasn't about me.

"It was an opportunity for our school. This is the wave of the future. It also allowed us to secure additional funding in state grants. The teachers were all behind it." Mr. Pfeiffer's lips pressed into a straight line. He looked away, as if to call on someone else but he hadn't finished answering everything yet.

"And about the teacher training?" I pressed. It was hard to copy his words into my notebook as I spoke. I looked up.

Mr. Pfeiffer had an unsure expression on his face. "I think that . . . ah . . . this is a work in progress and we will be supporting the teachers all the way along."

Ooh! I'd just found the weak spot in all this!

"So it's kind of on-the-job training?" I summarized. Outside, I was cool as a cucumber, but inside I was shaking like a leaf.

Mr. Pfeiffer's face hardened. "The teachers are being given every kind of help that they need. Next question?" He looked around the audience and called on a teacher who asked something easy. I sat down.

"What was that all about?" Michael asked in a whisper. He looked kind of mad.

I was fired up, though, so I didn't really care. "I just had a sense that that part of it hasn't been thought through all that well. And I was right."

"Wow. You were pretty harsh though, pressing him like that. You don't want to alienate a source before the article is finished."

"News is news. We need to present all the facts."

Michael looked at me like he was just really seeing me for the first time. I couldn't tell if it was in a good way or a bad way. I looked away and busied myself with copying down notes in my notebook. Did Michael think I'd gone too far? Had I? Did I care?

My stomach chose that moment to wail in protest of its hunger. I clamped my hand over it and felt my face turn beet red. I didn't know what to do. Should I acknowledge it or just pretend it hadn't happened?

There was a long moment where I had the sinking feeling that I'd just completely turned Michael off with my aggressive questioning and now with my noisy body. As my adrenaline wore off and my hands steadied, doubt began to creep in. I had a sinking feeling that Michael was angry with me.

But suddenly Michael was nudging me in the ribs. I looked over and he was holding a granola bar. Okay, now I was totally mortified that he had heard my stomach. But maybe this meant he didn't think I was an awful person for grilling Mr. Pfeiffer.

I looked up at his face and he was smiling. "Go on. Take it," he said, wiggling it at me. I palmed it from him and casually opened the wrapper. I broke off half the bar and handed him back the other half, but he waved it at me. I was so ravenous I could barely contain myself, but I didn't want to look like a pig, guinea or otherwise.

"Thanks," I whispered, taking a bite. Unfortunately it was the hard kind, so I had to kind of suck on the bite for a while to soften it up. I didn't want to make a racket sitting there eating Michael's snack.

Mr. Pfeiffer was now discussing how the curriculum changes would affect state testing. I copied down a few more choice quotes and started to get bored. Now that I had asked my questions and had a little snack, I was starting to feel tired, but I couldn't leave until the meeting was over. What if I missed something?

Michael nudged me again. "Hey. I'll follow up on that state funding he was talking about."

"What?" It rang a bell but I wasn't sure what he meant. I flipped through my notes but I couldn't find any reference to it.

Michael rolled his eyes at my notebook. "I'm going to head out," he said.

I was surprised that he would bail before the end of the meeting. "Really? Things aren't even close to over," I replied.

"The good stuff is," he whispered with a shrug. "Later, Crunchy." And he stood up and left.

Crunchy?! Aargh! Just what I need. Another nickname!

And the worst part was, Michael was right. The rest of the meeting was boring. At the very end it kind of fell apart with people arguing but not in an interesting way. Everyone pretty much stood up and left, and there was no change or resolution in the end. The new curriculum was here to stay and everyone was just going to have to get used to it.

I had wasted an extra hour trying to get more scoop, but it was Michael who had the real nose for news, knowing when to pull the rip cord and just bail. Annoying.

I was now late for dinner, behind on my homework, and I hadn't started the Dear Know-It-All column. I comforted myself by thinking back to Mr. Bloom, one of my teachers at journalism camp. He used to say 99 percent of being a journalist is just waiting around for something to happen. For the second half of tonight's meeting, he was right.

Chapter 9

GIRL GENIUS STRIKES AGAIN

★ ★ ★

I was up early the next day, sifting through my usual news haunts and checking my e-mail. There was one from Mr. Trigg, without anything in the subject line.

I clicked on it and read it. It said, "Samantha, hello. How is the new column coming along? I'd like to see a draft by Tuesday. Mr. T."

I gulped. A draft? I hadn't even decided for sure on the question yet and here it was, Friday! I slid out the packet of letters from behind my desk, where it was hiding. There were seven in total because I'd picked up four more yesterday.

Some were a little too heavy to deal with (like the bad home-life guy), especially for the firs column of the year. Some were dumb (a girl who can't remember her locker code). The one that kept drawing me back was the one from the guy who had a crush on his best friend's crush. I knew it would be a superpopular topic, and I wanted to lead the year with something hot. But what advice would I give? I couldn't even figure out my own crush!

I clicked back on Mr. Trigg's e-mail and hit reply. "Okay," I typed. That was all. I pressed send and bit my lip. As a total spazz in the romance department, I was really unqualified to answer this question. But whom could I ask for advice?

There was a knock on the door. "Mom told me to make sure you're up!"

Bingo!

I quickly closed my computer and stashed my envelope of letters, then I bounced over to the door and flung it open. Allie looked surprised to see me all bright-eyed so early in the morning. She had obviously assumed I was still asleep.

"Allie," I said seriously. "I have a question for you. It's . . . uh . . . it's part of something . . . something . . . we're working on in the new curriculum!" Eureka! *Girl Genius Strikes Again,* I thought. I smiled my most winning smile.

Allie looked at me suspiciously and folded her arms. "Okay . . ."

"What should someone do when he has a crush on the same girl his best friend likes?" I asked.

Allie's eyebrows knit together. "This is for school?"

"Yeah." I nodded. "It's . . . like a role-playing thing in our humanities class."

"Okay. Well, I know someone that that happened to . . ."

I knew I'd asked the right person! "And?"

"Well, there's really no right or wrong way to proceed in this situation," said Allie.

Wait, what? "But I need a concrete answer, fact based, you know? I have to, like, pick a side. Go for it or back off, buddy. Which one is it?"

Allie shrugged. "It's not that easy. You have to really look at all the factors. How important is the friendship? Is the crush really worth it?" Just then her phone buzzed and she answered.

Ugh! "Hello? We are talking here!" I said, annoyed.

Allie pressed the phone to the side of her head

and put her finger in her other ear to block me out. Then she turned away to walk to her room.

I found myself standing alone in the hall in my pj's.

Great. Nothing like being the least important person in someone's life.

I was dissatisfied with Allie's answer but I didn't have a better one myself. Maybe I should just pick a different question, I thought as I headed off to the shower.

TGIF! After my last class, I went to the newspaper office to check my mailbox (desperate to find a new letter that would be positively awesome for my column) before I left the building to meet Hailey down at the soccer field. I was sleeping over at her house tonight and was really looking forward to it. I felt like I hadn't seen her for days. I'd been so engrossed in reporting the curriculum article, typing up the soccer tryouts article, and trying to stay on top of my confusing new homework. Plus, tracking cutie Michael Lawrence whenever I had the chance!

And speak of the devil! I pushed open the office

door and instantly heard Michael's laughter. Yay! I had worn a new top today that Mom bought me that even Allie said looked nice. I was beginning to think Michael would never get to see me in it!

Inside I saw him and Jeff Perry leaning over the art director's large computer monitor. They looked up.

"Sammy! C'mere! You've gotta see this!" said Jeff, laughing and waving me over.

They were looking at photos Jeff had taken at the PTA meeting.

"Here. Check out Pfeiff," he said.

The picture opened up huge on the screen and it was a picture of Mr. Pfeiffer sitting quietly on the stage. Unfortunately, his hand was up at a weird angle and it looked exactly like he was picking his nose.

"Isn't that killer?" said Michael.

Jeff tried to look modest. "'Pfeiffer Picks a New Curriculum'?" he said with a shrug and a smile.

Mr. Trigg walked in and called out a greeting. "Happy weekend and all that!" he said.

Jeff and Michael looked at each other. "Show him," said Michael.

"Show me what, old chaps?" Mr. Trigg crossed

the room and came to stand behind the monitor. "Oh. That is rather unfortunate," he said.

"There are a few other good ones," said Jeff proudly. He scrolled through three more of Mr. Pfeiffer, one where he looked like he was going to throw up, one where Jeff had caught him with his eyes mid-blink so he looked like he was falling asleep in his chair, and one that was just kind of an ugly, unflattering shot.

"Well, you certainly managed to catch Mr. Pfeiffer at some awkward moments. You have quite the quick shutter speed, Jeff. Let's see some of the good ones, though."

Jeff looked up at him, his hand still on the mouse. "These are the good ones."

Mr. Trigg shook his head. "No, I mean the ones that we'll be choosing from to run with the article."

"That's what these are. I've narrowed it down. 'Pfeiffer Asleep at the Switch,' 'Pfeiffer Picks a Choice New Curriculum,' and 'Pfeiffer Sick of the Complaints.' Those are the captions."

Mr. Trigg was quiet for an extralong minute and we all got serious because we realized he was not happy. "Jeff, gang, stop for a moment. Think about what we are here for." He looked at the three of us carefully, eye to eye. Jeff shifted uncomfortably. After a long pause, Mr. Trigg continued. "Are we here to report the news? Or are we here to make people look like fools?" He looked around at us again. "I think you know the answer to that. We are not a tabloid, going for the quick laugh or the hurtful moment, are we?"

I shook my head no, and finally, so did Jeff and Michael.

"Mr. Pfeiffer may be a public figure, of sorts, and so technically he is fair game. But to make a mockery of him takes away from the hard reporting about the facts that I know Michael and Samantha are doing. We must treat our subjects respectfully and be mindful of our own credibility. These photos do tell a story of sorts, but they are not the story we are reporting. They are a sideshow. Do you all understand the difference?"

We nodded. I think Jeff felt bad. Not that he felt sorry for Mr. Pfeiffer but more that he was embarrassed that Mr. Trigg might think he was doing a bad job as photo editor. I looked at Michael. I wasn't sure he felt bad.

Mr. Trigg looked around again. "Would you like a bad photo of you out there for all the world to see? Maybe on Buddybook?"

I looked at Michael and saw that Mr. Trigg had just driven his point home. Michael felt bad now too, I could tell. I wondered if Mr. Trigg had seen Jeff's page when the football pictures were up. I wondered if he'd heard about Jeff's almost-fight with Andy Ryan.

Jeff clicked on the thumbnails of the bad photos of Mr. Pfeiffer and quietly dragged them into the computer's garbage can.

"Well done," said Mr. Trigg. Then he continued in an upbeat voice. "Now. Any fun weekend plans? I, for one, am off to hear a talk on Winston Churchill by a visiting professor from Oxford! Can't wait!"

I smiled. Good old Trigger. "Have fun!" I said.

Mr. Trigg left with a "Cheerio!" and Michael looked at his watch and announced it was time for football practice. Jeff was still sitting at the computer, looking thoughtful.

"You okay, bud?" asked Michael. "He wasn't mad at you or anything."

Jeff sighed. "I know. I just hate to waste a good photo."

"I hear you," said Michael.

"Do you think I should put them on Buddybook?" asked Jeff hopefully.

"No," Michael and I said in unison, then we laughed.

"Okay. Emptying trash," said Jeff with a sigh, clicking a few keys. "Have a good weekend, guys."

I realized Michael and I were leaving at the same time and probably heading in the same general direction.

"So guess what?" said Michael as we left.

"What?"

"I did an Internet search on the state funding that Mr. Pfeiffer got for the new curriculum." He had a small smile on his face.

"And?"

"And it's a little sketchy."

"What! No way!" Of course I was paying such close attention to Michael that I wasn't looking where

I was going. Someone must've spilled something on the floor and I slid in the puddle. "Whoa!" I yelled, clutching his sleeve to keep from wiping out.

I steadied myself without actually falling. "Sorry," I muttered, letting go of Michael's sleeve.

"I think we need to change your name to Trippy! Forget all the other nicknames!"

"Thanks," I said, annoyed. "So what did you find out? How much money is it? What's it for?" I was excited! This was like real reporting stuff.

"Down, Trippy!" said Michael, holding out a hand and laughing. "I'm not really sure. I need to show it to my dad and have him explain it to me. But it looks like the money is for the teachers, to develop the curriculum. Not really for the students."

"Wow." That could be an interesting angle to the story. "*Pfeiffer Secures Funds for Teachers, Not Kids,*" I said, trying it out. "Keep me posted."

"I still need to get a quote from Mrs. Jones," said Michael. "Then I'm pretty much done."

"Yeah, I just need a teacher quote. I'm going to ask Mrs. Frosch and then it's all wrapped up."

We had reached the boys' locker room. I stood

there feeling a little awkward all of a sudden. The idea of kissing him good-bye flitted through my head and I was mortified that I'd even thought it! I prayed Michael couldn't read minds.

"So we need to get together and write the thing," said Michael.

"Yeah." The idea of getting together with Michael was very appealing.

"Let's meet at the library next week. Tuesday? Fourth period like last week?"

I nodded, allowing myself to imagine Michael was asking me on a real date. I felt all swoony inside.

"I'll wear a suit of armor and bring lots of food," he said. "I don't want to get hurt and I know how hungry you get. See ya, Trippy!" And he went in the door.

My bubble was totally burst. I had made an impression all right. But Michael hadn't noticed my new shirt. He noticed that I was a klutz. Right then I hated him.

Chapter 10

MURDER ON THE SOCCER FIELD

I stomped down to the bleachers by the soccer field. Michael Lawrence was a jerk! Why was he always ragging on me? I didn't stand a chance with him. He thought I was a klutzy, overeating idiot!

I slammed my messenger bag down on the bench and sat down heavily next to it. Hailey looked over and waved. Thank goodness for Hailey. Boys were too confusing, and friends were the only people you could count on in life. *Girl* friends!

"Hey!" called Hailey from the field. I guess I was reading more than watching and hadn't noticed practice was over. I jump-stepped down from the bleachers and over to Hailey. She was all sweaty.

"Hi. How was practice?" I asked, not really interested.

"Awesome! Our coach went to a training camp this summer and she has all these new drills and . . ." I hate to say it but I tuned Hailey out and just let her talk. I could never be a sportswriter (my soccer tryouts article focused on the human element and the numbers, not the moves). In the end, who really cares? It's just a game.

The football team was coming in and they caught my eye as they crossed the soccer field to hit the locker room. I quickly looked away and averted my eyes from number fifteen. Let him think I didn't see him. I had nothing to say to Michael Lawrence right now.

But apparently Hailey did. "Hey, fifteen!" she called. Michael broke from the line and walked over to us.

Ugh. "Hailey!" I whispered in my meanest whisper. But she ignored me.

"How was practice?" she asked as he drew near.

"Hey, Hailey. What's up, Trippy?" he said.

I rolled my eyes and didn't reply.

Those two got chatting about drills and new kinds of stretching while I busied myself with checking my to-do list in my notebook.

I looked up, and Hailey had found a soccer ball and was doing this thing where she tries to see how many times she can bounce it off her foot and head and knee without it touching the ground. "Juggling," she was calling it. I was a little bit proud of her because she is very, very good at it. She could do it so many times in a row.

Michael clapped. "Way to go!" he said. "Here, let me try!"

Hailey booted it over to him and he caught it with his foot, then he started doing the juggling thing. He got to fourteen and lost the ball. Then Hailey said, "I can beat that!" and gave it another try.

I sighed in irritation. This was boring and I hated Michael. "Hailey, let's *go*," I said.

Michael looked over at me. "In a rush?"

I shrugged.

"No," said Hailey.

Murder on the Soccer Field, I thought. Couldn't she tell I wanted to get out of here?

Hailey got to twenty-seven juggles, or whatever they were called, and Michael whistled with his fingers in his mouth. I love when guys can do that, even though I hate Michael.

"Hey, Pasty, you try," he said. Oh great, now we're back to the original.

"No, I . . ." But Hailey had already booted me the ball. I tried to reach it but I slid and went kind of sprawling. My bag swung forward and I tipped over. My face burned as I stood up and those two were laughing.

"Does she do this all the time?" Michael asked Hailey.

"That's why we love her!" replied Hailey.

I picked myself up and adjusted my bag, which had flopped open. Fine. I can play at this game. I pulled the ball over with my toe and gave it a few little kicks. It kind of hurt. I bent down to lift it and start it off in the air, but they both hollered, "No hands!"

I dropped it like a hot potato. "Chillax!" I said. Sheesh.

I wiggled the ball around and got it in the air. I managed two juggles a few times and once even three, but there was no way I was getting as many as those two.

They called out tips and encouragement, and I wasn't sure if it would be worse to quit or keep trying and failing. Finally, I booted the ball back to Hailey.

"We have our work cut out for us tonight," she said.

"Yeah," I said, even crankier. As if I was going to spend quality sleepover time learning soccer moves!

"Well, let me know if you ever need some extra help coaching," said Michael.

Hailey laughed. "I need all the help I can get!"

"That's not what it looked like yesterday!"

"Well, that was just a casual scrimmage," said Hailey. "Next time I'll really take you down!"

Michael laughed. "I dare you!"

Wait, were these guys flirting? I looked at Hailey and she was flushed. She fluffed her hair and smiled at Michael really big. He smiled back.

"What was yesterday?" I asked, as casually as I could manage.

"Oh, we just had a friendly shoot-out after practice," said Hailey.

"It wasn't so friendly, actually," Michael said with a laugh.

"Well that's your own fault, trash-talking me like that." Hailey wagged her finger at him.

"Yo, Lawrence! Chalk talk!" A coach shouted from the locker room door. Michael looked at him and waved.

"Gotta go," Michael said.

"See ya!" said Hailey, really energetically.

"Bye!" replied Michael. "Later, Paste," he said to me, and gave me a salute before he jogged off.

Paste? Now my nickname had a nickname?

I looked at Hailey. She was laughing to herself and shaking her head as she scooped up the ball with her toe.

"Are you laughing at my nickname?" I asked. I felt really annoyed with her but I couldn't exactly say why. If I had to break it down, I guess it was because they had kind of left me out of that whole conversation in a way, even though they were talking to me. It was weird.

"What? No! I just . . . He's funny."

"Humph," I said crankily.

I was thinking about them having a scrimmage and how neither of them had mentioned it before.

And it had been yesterday. Which meant that while I had been waiting at the PTA meeting for Michael to come meet me, he was playing soccer with Hailey! Now I was even madder at him than before!

"Let's hit it. I can shower at home," said Hailey.

I looked at her long and hard. Was there something up with her and Michael?

No. No way.

But it was annoying that they had that whole sporty, jokey thing going. Really annoying.

It wasn't until much later that night that I realized I'd lost my notebook. I couldn't believe it. I went to my bag to write down an idea I had for the curriculum article, and the notebook wasn't there. It must've fallen out of my messenger bag back when I wiped out at the field.

I felt sick.

Hailey and I were already in our pj's and had mud masks on our faces. I couldn't even scream because my face would crack.

"I ost i ote-ook," I said to Hailey desperately.

"Ut?" she asked. She looked at me in confusion.

"I *ost* i *ote*-ook!"

There was a pause. Then Hailey figured it out.

"Ait! Ur *OTE*-ook?" She mimed writing on a pad of paper.

"Ess!" I nodded emphatically.

We only had a little more time left on the masks so it did seem like a shame after having that stuff on for twenty minutes to wash it off with only a few minutes more to go. But Hailey is a good friend and she understands how much I rely on my notebook for everything.

"Et's awsh ih ah," she said generously.

After we were all clean, Hailey got her dad and some flashlights, and the three of us went back to the soccer field where I had wiped out and my bag had opened. We looked all around there and then expanded our search to the bleachers and everything, and it was just plain gone.

I probably would have kept looking all night, as if the looking would magically make it appear, but I felt bad for Hailey and her dad, so I told them it was okay and that we could leave.

"I'm sorry, Sammy," said Hailey when we got back to the car.

I shrugged hopelessly. Everything was in there. My story ideas, quotes from the PTA meeting, to-do lists, homework assignments, everything. I was pretty devastated. The only silver lining was that I didn't have anything incriminating about my crush on Michael or my Know-It-All column. Thank goodness! As much as writing is my life, it's always important to know what you *shouldn't* put in writing.

Hailey suggested we go on her page on Buddybook and post a notice that I had lost my notebook at school and if anyone finds it, to please return it to us. I thought that was really nice of her.

Once she was logged in and had her page up, I sat beside her while she typed the notice.

"Want to go look at some pages while we're on here?" she asked, with a mischievous twinkle in her eye.

"Oh, what the heck. Sure." I didn't want to be a total stick in the mud, especially when

Hailey was being so nice.

"Hmmm . . . How about Jeff Perry's? He usually has some hilarious photo up there," offered Hailey.

But Jeff didn't have much up. I think he'd been properly scolded by Trigger and it would take a while before he'd post anything mean again.

We looked at some girls' pages—leaving notes for the girls we were friends with and laughing at the pages of girls we don't like.

It was actually really fun.

"Thanks, Hailey," I said, feeling a warm glow of friendship love. "You're the best friend ever."

"I try," said Hailey, fluffing her hair in a kind of joking, modest way.

There was one page we hadn't visited, and I was still so sick of him that I didn't want to ask to go there. But I wouldn't say no if Hailey offered. Which, of course, being the good friend that she is, she did.

"Want to see Michael Lawrence's page?" she asked, giggling.

I shrugged. "Eh . . . whatever. I'm so over him right now."

"*Really*," said Hailey in more of a statement than a question.

"He's just been a bit of a pain lately," I said. But I was still glued to his page when Hailey navigated to it. I couldn't help it. The boy was cute.

"Do you still like him?" Hailey asked. She was peering closely at his photo but her voice was kind of weird.

"Yeah! Duh!"

She looked at me and smiled, but it was kind of a sad smile, like she understood that you could be into someone in general but also not be into him right at that very moment.

"Wait, can I just slide over here and get a little closer look?" I asked, nudging Hailey off her desk chair.

"You know what? Sit here and I'll go downstairs and get some more snacks. Okay?"

"Okay, best friend. Thanks," I said, and she left.

I looked at his cute picture on his home page and noted his status—single! I wanted to click on his wall but Hailey has a tracking pad, which I'm not used to, so my finger kind of slipped and I wound up clicking on a document on her desktop.

"Ack! Cancel, cancel!" I tried to stop the computer from opening Word, but I was stuck in the process. It was too late. I sighed and sat back, waiting until it was completely open so I could close it and quit the application. Only what appeared before me made my mouth drop open and my heart stop beating.

It couldn't be!

Chapter 11

GIRL LEAVES BEST FRIEND'S HOUSE– FOREVER!

★ ★ ★

There it was, right in front of me. At first, I wondered how Hailey had gotten a copy of it.

I was that confused.

Then I realized the truth.

Hey Mr. Know-It-All,

What do you do when you and your best friend have a crush on the same person?

Signed,
Unlucky Taste

Hailey was Unlucky Taste.

I sat there dumbstruck for a second. I think my jaw even dropped. But then I heard Hailey saying something to her dad and I knew she must be at the foot of the stairs. I scrambled to close the document and quit the application. *Why are computers so slow?!*

"Close, close, close! Hurry!" I whispered hard at the computer. I even blew on it, as if that would help. ***Computer Hacker Caught in the Act.***

Just as I heard Hailey's footsteps at the top of the stairs, the application closed, and I was able to click back onto Michael's Buddybook page. I adjusted my features. All I felt was shock, but I couldn't let Hailey see it on my face. Especially because I hadn't begun to process all that her letter meant.

"Here we go!" Hailey sang, coming into the room with a plate of cookies and two milks.

"The cookies are made with spelt flour, sweetened with agave nectar. They have dried cherries and pistachios in them. And here"—she offered me my glass of milk—"skim and organic, baby, with extra vitamin D!"

I was glad for the distraction. I selected a cookie and took a careful nibble. It wasn't bad. Then I took a swig of milk and carefully eyed Hailey over the rim of the glass, my face hidden from sight by all that milk.

Hailey had no idea what I now knew. And I couldn't imagine how I was going to get through the rest of the night pretending like nothing had happened.

"Oh, hey! I have a new message! Oh look! It's from Michael!" Hailey's face was glowing and her smile beaming so wide it practically touched both of her ears. How could I not have noticed before that she loved him? Am I a total idiot?

Then I had a sickening thought: *What if he liked her back?!*

I felt like I'd been punched in the stomach. Bad enough to have your best friend betray you by falling in love with your lifelong crush, but to have the crush like her back?! Oh my goodness! My face burned hot but my body felt cold. I was in a full panic.

"Let's see . . . What does he say . . ." Hailey was clicking around Buddybook happily. No wonder she was all up-to-date on that cute photo Jeff had posted of Michael at football practice. I was surprised it wasn't *her* screensaver!

"Yay! Sammy, he has your notebook! He says, 'Tell Pasty I found her notebook. If she gives me a call, we can arrange a drop-off,' and then it has his phone number. Hey! We should call him!" Hailey turned to me with a look of excitement on her face. "Want to?" she added.

Now I was starting to understand. I was kind of the pawn in her crush. She could use me as the buffer or the go-between, as an excuse to check in on Michael and talk to him and everything. Like she's reporting back to me, but it's really for her.

"No," I said in as flat of a voice as I could manage.

"What?" Hailey looked surprised. I think she'd been assuming I'd say yes.

I felt a mean prick of pleasure at having burst her bubble. Ha! Take that! I'm not going to be your excuse to call your lover boy. No way.

"Why?" she asked again, kind of forlorn.

I shrugged, relishing my power. "I'm tired. I just want to go to sleep. I'll deal with it in the morning. Anyway, he'll probably have read through the whole thing and he'll have something mean to say about my reporting skills and my to-do lists. It's all just . . . embarrassing. Why did it have to be him who found it?"

Hailey was reluctant to give up. "All right. If you say so . . ."

"I say so. Plus, he'd just tease me and call me Listy or Trippy or Pasty or one of those annoying nicknames."

Hailey bit her lip and was quiet for a minute. "At least you *have* nicknames from him."

That made me mad. "What? You'd like your lifelong crush to call you insulting names based on your personality flaws or mistakes you made when you were five? *That's* fun," I said bitterly.

Hailey shrugged. "Okay, maybe not *those* names . . ."

"Yeah . . ." I said, nodding hard, "definitely not *those* names."

I kind of hated Hailey right then. I almost wanted to tell her flat out that I knew she loved Michael too and that she couldn't have him. But then I'd have to leave, and since it was eleven o'clock, that would not be easy to pull off.

"I think we should just go to sleep," I said.

Hailey raised her eyebrows. "O-kayyy . . ." she said. Eleven was early for us on a sleepover.

"I have a lot of work to do tomorrow." I shrugged and rummaged in my overnight bag for my toothbrush. Inside, I was furious.

Hailey was bummed. This night hadn't turned out so well, but it was kind of her fault, even though she didn't know it. Whatever. It might be the last sleepover we ever have, anyway.

"Fine," said Hailey.

We were asleep ten minutes later. Or at least, she was. I hardly slept a wink all night.

The next morning I just wanted to get out of there. I called my mom first thing and she said she'd be over to pick me up at nine. I figured I should pick up my notebook on the way home, so I asked Hailey for Michael's number from the Buddybook page and she was all too eager to get it for me. She offered to dial and ask for him, but I had to silence her with a glare and do it myself. Now that I knew for a fact that she liked him, all of her actions took on a new significance and she was getting more annoying by the minute.

I was nervous to call him but my eagerness to get my notebook back as well as my aggravation with the two of them empowered me. I punched in the numbers and prepared myself to get an answering machine.

"Hello?"

Oh. I hadn't had a moment to compose myself and Michael was already on the phone.

"Hi, Michael. It's Sam."

"Hey, Pasty. Calling about your notebook?"

I rolled my eyes and gritted my teeth. "Yup."

"You must be lost without it. I was flipping through it and that's . . . that's a lot of information you've got in there."

Great. He was flipping through it. "Yup," I said, wondering how much he had read. "So where should I meet you to get it back?"

"Oh. Well, I'm at home now for a little while before my game. You could come here, or I could drop it by later . . ."

"I'll come by," I said. "My mom is picking me up from Hailey's house in a few minutes, so we could be over soon."

"Great! Okay! So I'll see you soon!" He sounded pretty chipper.

"Okay. Bye." I hung up.

There was a thick silence in the kitchen and I didn't know how to break it. Finally, Hailey did.

"You didn't even thank him," she said quietly.

"What?" I had no idea what she was talking about.

"Well, he found your notebook for you. You . . . you should have thanked him. I mean, you'd be lost without it, right?"

She was right. I felt my face grow warm, but I quickly got mad that Hailey was bossing me around all the time now.

"I'll thank him when I see him," I said. "Anyway, why do you care?"

Hailey shrugged. "I just don't think you're very nice to him."

"So?"

"He's pretty nice to you . . ." Hailey said.

"Not really," I said sarcastically.

"Oh, whatever!" Hailey was annoyed now, and on one level, I didn't blame her. I was acting pretty mean and cranky and she had no idea why. But the rest of me felt like: Too bad! You lovebirds are ruining my life and I hate you both!

There was a honk outside and I looked out the window. It was my mom in her Jeep, here to pick me up.

"Well . . . thanks," I said.

"Yeah, anytime," Hailey said, not that nicely.

I sighed and picked up my bag.

"Say hi to lover boy for me," she said as I left.

Yeah, right. "Okay," I said. "See you later!" And I closed the door behind me.

Chapter 12

MARTONE DISTRAUGHT OVER TURN OF EVENTS

★ ★ ★

My mom was happy to see me, if a little perplexed because I usually just stay all day after a sleepover. But I explained about my notebook and I played the workload card and she bought it.

We were at Michael's house in less than two minutes, and my mom pulled up at the curb so I could run to the door.

I climbed the steps to the front porch and reached out to ring the doorbell, but the door flung open and Michael was standing there, freshly showered (yet again), in a faded green T-shirt and old jeans. He looked gorgeous. It kind of took my breath away for a minute.

"H-hi," I stammered. I felt supershy and

overwhelmed seeing him looking so good and being at his house and everything. It was different than running into him at school.

Michael grinned. "Hi. I saw you pull up. Cool Jeep."

I looked over my shoulder. "Thanks. It's my mom's."

"Cool mom," he said.

I nodded. "Most of the time."

"Want to come in?" he asked, opening the door wide and gesturing with his arm.

"Oh . . . uh . . . no thanks. I . . ." I peeked in and I could see a really pretty hallway with striped wallpaper. Plus an amazing cinnamon smell was coming from the kitchen. I was dying to go in and look all around. But I felt so awkward. It was weird enough being at his front door, never mind touring around the house. Plus Mom was sitting in the car. "Oh! Well, my mom is waiting."

"Mikey?" It must have been his mom calling from the kitchen. "I think your cinnamon buns are ready!" She came walking out, her low heels clicking on the hardwood floor. Michael's mom is really pretty. I've seen her before. She's a lot older than my mom but still really pretty, with that same tan skin and dark hair, and the same light eyes that he has. "Hi!" she said with a big, friendly smile. "You must be Samantha!"

I smiled back and held out my hand. I was really nervous, like more nervous than I'd been before. "Hi. It's nice to meet you," I said, shaking her hand.

"Oh, such good manners! I'm glad Mikey found your notebook! I'd die if I lost my FiloFax, where I keep everything!"

I nodded. "I know. Thanks so much," I said to him, finally. "Really! I really appreciate it." I thought about what Hailey said and winced. "I was worried all night, so . . . really, thanks."

"Oh, it's no big deal. I know how attached you are to that thing. And when the coach had me run out to pick up the cones, I saw it just lying there in the grass where we'd been juggling, so . . ." He shrugged.

His mom looked back and forth between us and smiled. "Maybe I'll go grab the cinnamon buns so they don't burn. Would you like to come and have some? Mikey just made them, especially . . ."

"Okay, Mom. Thanks!" Michael interrupted her. "Kitchen. Burning buns! Thanks!" He waved her away.

"Bye, Samantha! It was nice to meet you!" She waved and ran off.

Michael rolled his eyes and shook his head. "Mothers!" he said, embarrassed.

I looked at him. "What are you baking for?" I asked. He was so manly; I couldn't picture him baking anything. This was like a whole new side of Michael Lawrence.

His face turned red. "Oh, nothing. I just . . . you know. They're really tasty. Are you sure you wouldn't like one? Are you sure you don't want to come in?"

I felt so shy and nerdy it was almost physically painful. I just wanted to get out of there at that point and put myself out of this miserable awkwardness. But at the same time, Michael Lawrence was inviting me in for a snack! Ha! Take that, Hailey!

I glanced out to my mom in the Jeep. She waved and smiled. Michael waved back.

"I think I'd better go . . ." I said reluctantly.

"Okay, that's fine! Totally! I understand. You

probably have a million things to do today. So. Okay. Let me just grab . . ." Michael awkwardly tried to stretch to the hall table while still holding the door but it wasn't going to work.

"Here," I offered. I stuck my foot out to prop open the door as he reached for the notebook.

"Hey, Pasty," he joked, "careful with that door near my hand!"

I must have turned bright red. "Oh!" I said, and pulled my foot back fast.

"I was kidding!" said Michael, handing me the notebook.

"Right. Well, thank you so, so much," I said. "Really, I can't thank you enough." Somehow I felt bad about not coming in. Like I was even being a little rude, as if I'd been expected.

It seemed like neither of us knew what to do next.

"Well, bye!" I said. I turned away but Michael's mom came running to the door.

"Wait! Samantha! You've got to try one of Mikey's cinnamon buns! He makes the best!"

"Mom!" Michael protested. He was mortified, I could tell.

She handed me a pretty paper napkin with a big, squishy cinnamon bun that was dripping with frosting.

"Wow!" I said. I was impressed. "You made this?" I asked Michael.

He nodded.

"Yum! Thanks! Thank you both, so much, for everything!" I said. "See you!"

"Bye!" Michael and his mom stood in the doorway and waved as I walked back to the Jeep. I waved back and then got in.

"Yum!" said my mom, looking at the bun.

"I know," I said. "Total yum!"

The bun was delicious. One of the best things I've ever eaten, actually. It was gone before I even got home. As I licked the gooey white frosting from my fingers, I thought back to what Michael's mom had been about to say, about Michael making them especially for something. I wondered what for.

At my desk at home, I laid out all of the Dear Know-It-All letters. There were ten in all. The most recent were about someone whose mom wouldn't let them drink soda (boring), juggling homework loads (two of them, so double boring), and one about what to do when your socks fall down all the time in gym (Really? Buy new socks). I was stuck with Hailey's letter. It was the only decent one to tackle as the first column of the year. It set the right tone, it had spunk, and it was exciting. It was also about me and, oh yeah, one little detail: I had no idea how to answer it.

I looked at it with everything I was feeling: shock, anger, disappointment, jealousy. Most of all I felt mad. It was making me feel jangly. What could I possibly say to her?

Dear Unlucky,

Go find a new friend. Just make sure you don't ruin her life too.

From,
Dear Know-It-All

Or how about this?:

Dear Hailey,

I hate you.

From,
Sam

That would be pretty direct.

I was paralyzed. I scooped the letters back up and shoved them haphazardly into the envelope. Maybe I could tell Mr. Trigg that he had picked the wrong person for the job. He could switch to someone else before it was too late. Someone who knows how to actually give advice. Someone who knows what to say to a boy or how to not fall down in front of him. I was better at facts than feelings. Facts were black and white. Feelings were all sorts of colors.

But somehow I knew if I copped out now, my shot at editor in chief would be over.

With a sigh, I opened a new page on my computer and started transcribing all of the material and quotations I'd gathered for my small soccer tryouts story and my huge curriculum story. It was going to be a long day.

Chapter 13

DEADLINE PANIC
SETS IN!

I avoided Hailey for the rest of the weekend, but when I came into homeroom on Monday morning, there she was, sitting on Michael's desk! They were chatting and laughing and didn't see me come in until I was right next to them in my row.

"Hi, Sam," said Hailey, spotting me first. She climbed down (good thing!) and went back to her seat in the next row.

"Hey, Pasty!" said Michael, smiling. He seemed happy to see me.

"Hey, Mikey!" I said. Two could play at this game.

He laughed. "Oh, please! Don't let that one follow me to school."

"Ha! See that! How does it feel?" I laughed,

pointing a finger at him. "Only if you promise no more Pasty!"

"Mikey?" asked Hailey, but I wasn't going to clue her in. I decided to work it a little.

"The cinnamon bun was amazing. Thank you."

Michael laughed. "I can't believe my mom basically chased you out the door with that thing!"

"What thing?" asked Hailey, but I ignored her. I don't think Michael actually heard her. So there! I decided to take it even further.

"I'm so sorry I couldn't stay. I had so much work this weekend, mostly for that article we're doing together." I sighed.

"Oh no, look . . . I totally understand. I had a lot too. We'll do it another time. Hey! Did I tell you I got my dad to look into that whole state funding thing? It turns out . . ."

Michael was really into it and telling me the whole story behind the curriculum change funding. Pfeiffer hadn't done anything wrong (I was kind of relieved about that, actually), just that he was kind of bending the truth to make things sound better. But I wasn't even really paying attention to what

Michael was saying. I had half an eye on Hailey and her reaction to our conversation.

I nodded as Michael talked, trying to look interested but also pretty at the same time. I flipped my hair, only once, but smoothed it down in long waves over my shoulder (you can't do that with a pixie cut, can ya, Hailey?). I kept my eyes on Michael and asked lots of questions. Two could play this game.

Finally, the teacher called the class to order.

"So we're meeting tomorrow, anyway, right?" I whispered loudly, so Hailey would hear.

"Yeah!" said Michael, smiling and seeming pumped about it. "It's going to be a great article!" he said.

I smiled and nodded, then I glanced at Hailey. She had a stony look on her face. I felt a tiny twinge bad, but hey. What could I do? She's the one who's after *my* established crush!

In math, though, Hailey passed me a note. It said: "Are you mad at me?"

Yet another note from Hailey that I didn't know how to answer.

At lunch I rushed to the *Voice* office. I didn't

want to deal with seating issues in the cafeteria (would I avoid Hailey?), and more importantly, I wanted to see if I'd received any new letters. I was desperate for something good that would save me from having to deal with Hailey's letter. But at the same time I really didn't want to run into Mr. Trigg. I knew the column should have been taking shape by now. It was due to him Tuesday so he could look it over before we went to press Thursday night. I wasn't giving him a whole lot of time and I knew that was not a great way to start off the column. Professionals (especially editors in chief) are never late for their deadlines.

I opened the door and peeked in. Phew! I didn't see Trigger!

"Hello, Samantha!"

Darn it! He was coming in right behind me!

"Hi, Mr. Trigg. Did you have a good weekend? How was the Churchill lecture? Was the guy interesting?" I had to keep him talking while I checked my mailbox.

"Oh, it was just wonderful! *Wonderful!* I learned some new facts I'd never known before. Time well spent. But more importantly, how are things going with the column?" Mr. Trigg lowered his voice to a whisper and looked over his shoulder as if someone else might be there.

Now what?

"Well, Mr. Trigg . . . I've been meaning to talk to you. The letters aren't great. There aren't really any that are *jazzy* enough for the first column. They're all pretty dumb." I gulped nervously as I lied.

Mr. Trigg folded his arms and reached up to tap his chin awkwardly. It was his trademark mannerism. "What about . . . I know there was one good one I saw. Was it? . . . Let me think." Tap, tap, tap.

Please don't let him say Hailey's, I thought desperately. But of course . . .

He thrust his finger in the air. "The crush! The crush on the best friend's crush! That's the ticket! It's perfect."

Ugh!

"But what do I tell her?" I said, trying not to whine.

"How do you know it's a her?" he asked, surprised.

"I mean, or him?" I corrected myself quickly.

"You just tell him or her . . . all's fair in love and war!"

I didn't like that answer. Not when it applied to Hailey. How could I write that?

Just then Michael Lawrence walked in and our discussion was over.

"Wednesday," said Mr. Trigg, pointing his finger at me. "Alrighty?"

I nodded, miserable. "Wednesday," I agreed.

Deadline Panic Sets In for New Columnist.

"What's Wednesday?" asked Michael, taking a bite of an apple. I was hungry and I sure wasn't about to stick around and let my stomach announce it.

"Oh, nothing, just brainstorming," I said in what I hoped was a breezy fashion.

"Speaking of which, maybe we should go over our notes now and use tomorrow to try to get in and get another quote from Pfeiffer," said Michael.

This guy was killing me! Here I am starving and in a rush and of *course* I'd kill to hang out with him, but talk about bad timing!

"Um . . . I was going to go grab some food in

the cafeteria right now," I said.

"I just ate, but I'm free," said Michael. He grinned. "Let's go feed you before your stomach starts yelling."

I was so embarrassed. "Yeah, I . . ." But I didn't know how to answer him. I didn't know how to answer anything these days.

"Hey, it's okay!" he said. "I always carry snacks with me. I get hungry all the time too!"

In the cafeteria Michael grabbed a table while I got my tray. It was hard to decide what to get. I didn't want to look like a pig in front of Michael, or get food caught in my teeth or make a mess. Finally, I made my selections and headed over to him and sat down. I pulled a sheaf of papers out of my messenger bag and laid it on the table.

"I transcribed my notes. Here's what I have," I said. "It looks like the theme is that everyone was caught off guard by the changes, the communication was poor in explaining it, but overall the kids and teachers are very happy with the new curriculum," I explained. "I think that's our thesis."

Michael was nodding. "I'd like to add in a big section that explains the changes, where we use Pfeiffer's quote about 'We'd also like you to be able to tell a great story, because isn't that what everything comes down to in life? Telling a great story?'"

"Wow. How do you remember just what he said?"

Michael shrugged. But he was smiling kind of proudly.

I was impressed but maybe kind of nervous. How did he know for sure that he'd gotten it word for word if he didn't write it down? Misquoting people is dangerous.

"I also think we should work in when he said at the PTA meeting 'this is a work in progress,'" Michael continued. "That could really be our thesis."

I flipped through the pages looking for that quote from when I asked the questions in the PTA meeting. "Oh, that sounds familiar, I just need to . . ."

Michael put his hand on top of mine to stop me from continuing to flip. "It's okay. I know he said it."

I stared at his hand. On mine. Then I looked up. He was looking at me and I was so overwhelmed by his cute but serious face that I had to quickly glance away. As I did, my eyes fell upon Hailey, who was eating lunch a few tables away, staring at us. She had such a sad look on her face that my first instinct was to drop everything and run over to her to see what was wrong. But then I remembered that she loved Michael and that I was mad at her, so I didn't do anything. I just looked back at him.

He looked at me and lifted his hand off mine, and as I pulled my hand back, I spilled my milk, of course, all over my tray. When I'd finished mopping it up, I looked around and Hailey was gone. A tiny part of me felt bad, but I pushed it away.

The spellbinding moment with Michael was broken, and now I was chattering a mile a minute in embarrassment, asking Michael all sorts of nervous questions about Pfeiffer.

"Listen," Michael said finally. "Just because you wrote something down doesn't mean you got it right either. You could have misheard him or your pen could slip and make it messy so you transcribe it wrong. The truth is subject to lots of variables."

"I guess," I said. "It's just that I love facts."

Michael laughed. "I know!"

He looks so cute when he laughs. His teeth are

so white and his eyes crinkle at the corners. I could just stare at his face all day long.

We quickly divided up the column and who would write which part, then we went down to the office to set up an appointment to meet Pfeiffer the next day for a quick follow-up.

Michael and I had to run off to our next classes but we agreed to e-mail each other our drafts of the story tonight, whatever we had.

"Hey, are you on Buddybook?" he asked.

"Nah . . . that thing is just a time waster."

Michael shrugged. "It can be a good way to take polls. Like if we set up a page to see who is for or against the curriculum and why."

Oh. Well. That would be handy. "Whatever you think . . ." I said.

He nodded briskly. "I'll give it a shot. See ya."

"See ya." I forced myself to turn away and not watch him go. What a cutie! *Journalist Drowns as Cowriter Drools all over Him.*

Chapter 14

PEACE ACHIEVED BY WARRING FACTIONS

At Mr. Pfeiffer's office the next morning, I clutched my draft of the article and reread it, kind of obsessively. I had to make sure everything was exactly right. I liked what we had, but until we were finished with our Pfeiffer meeting, I wouldn't be able to relax.

The phone on the secretary's desk buzzed and then she said, "Kids? He'll see you now."

This visit was clearly not going to be as warm and fuzzy as the last. We opened his door and went in.

"Hello," said Mr. Pfeiffer, standing up. "What can I help you with today?"

"Hi. Thanks for seeing us," Michael began. "We just wanted to tie up some loose end before we put the article to bed," I said.

Mr. Pfeiffer nodded. "Have a seat."

We sat and then Michael and I looked at each other. I gestured to him to talk first.

"Okay, first of all, I thought you'd like to know that I put up a Buddybook page on the curriculum changes and asked people to vote for or against it."

I looked at Pfeiffer. He was kind of wincing. I felt a little bad for him.

Michael pulled a sheet of paper out of his pocket. "And as of seven o'clock this morning, you had seven hundred seventy-two people in favor of it, and only three hundred twenty against it. So that's good news."

Pfeiffer allowed a small smile but he was still suspicious of us. He nodded. "Go on."

Michael continued. "I just wanted to get your comments on the state funding of the change. I pulled up these documents." He stood and laid them on Pfeiffer's desk. "They indicate that the funding for the changes was actually funding for teacher development that was kind of redirected to this project."

Pfeiffer sat up and flipped through the pages.

Then he looked up at us. "Impressive research." For the first time, he smiled. "I'm glad that our school newspaper staff is so dedicated."

"Can you explain the funding?" asked Michael.

Pfeiffer was relaxed now. "Yes. The way that money for public education is allocated is through a very political process involving budgets and unions. It can be ugly, sneaky, and disheartening. We have wanted to make these curriculum changes for a very long time but were unable to fight the teacher's union to get money for kids rather than the teachers. In the end, we were able to reach a compromise wherein the teachers technically got the money, but what it really was for was to teach them a new way of teaching. It allows them to explore more reading and writing-based materials and it supports them in their learning to teach in this new way. So while it looks kind of tricky on paper, it's just a back door way of getting the money we need but making everyone happy along the way. You know, sometimes in politics, like in life, not everything is black and white. Sometimes there are gray areas to consider."

Michael was the one who was impressed now, and I had to admit, I was too.

"So you kind of trick the government into giving you the money you want, for the project you want, and everyone ends up happy?"

Pfeiffer was beaming now. "Yes."

I made some notes and then it was my turn. "The other thing we were wondering about was when you said at the meeting that it's a 'work in progress,' do you think you should have waited to unveil the new curriculum until it was totally ready?"

Mr. Pfeiffer's face darkened, like a cloud passing over the sun. "I didn't say that," he said.

My heart skipped a beat. "Yes you did."

But Mr. Pfeiffer was shaking his head. "I never said such a thing. It's not true. We were all ready with the roll out."

Michael interrupted. "With all due respect, Mr. Pfeiffer, you did say it."

Pfeiffer was growing angry, I could see it. "Kids, I am all for encouraging young journalists, and I think Mr. Trigg is doing a terrific job with the paper. But putting words in my mouth is going too far. Now, I'm happy to answer any other questions you might have. I have"—he lifted his cuff and looked at his watch—"exactly two minutes until my next meeting, so is there anything else?"

Michael and I looked at each other. This was not good. A Work in Progress was going to be our headline.

Finally, Michael looked at Mr. Pfeiffer. "That's it, sir." He stood up and put his hand out for a handshake. "Thank you for your time."

"Glad to be helpful," said Mr. Pfeiffer gruffly.

"Thanks, Mr. Pfeiffer," I said.

In the hall I let out a huge sigh. "Phew. That was intense. What do you think?"

Michael rubbed his eyes and shook his head. "Man, I don't know. I remember him saying it. And it's such a bummer because that was our headline and our thesis."

"Back to the drawing board," I said.

"Ugh. I barely have any time tonight," said Michael.

"I can take a stab at reworking it," I said. "We sure can't put it in if he's denying saying it. I just wish we could prove it. I mean, facts are *facts*."

"Remember what he said, not everything is black and white. Sometimes there's a gray area to consider."

"Humph," I said. "There's no such thing as gray areas!"

Michael laughed. "I've gotta run. Let's touch base later."

I nodded. "Definitely."

He went one way and I went the other, and who should I bump into, literally, but Hailey.

"Oh my goodness. Sorry!" I said, bending to pick up the book I'd knocked out of her hand. I handed it back to her and our eyes met. Hailey looked miserable. I didn't know what to say.

"Why didn't you answer my note the other day?" she asked.

"What note?" I said, but as I spoke I remembered. Darn! "Oh. I just . . . I didn't know what to say."

"Well, *are* you mad at me?" she asked.

"I . . . I'm not mad. No. I'm just . . . frustrated. That's all."

Hailey almost looked relieved. "Why? What did I do?" she asked.

I sighed. Nothing. Everything. How could I possibly explain? "It's nothing . . . black or white," I said, trying out Mr. Pfeiffer's figure of speech. "It's just . . . I don't know. I was kind of annoyed over the weekend."

Hailey looked perplexed. "Well, are you still?"

I took a deep breath and let it out. "I guess not." Not on an everyday basis, anyway. I'd spent so much quality time with Michael during the past few days that I didn't really feel like Hailey was ahead anymore in the fight for his love. Plus, let's face it, she was my best friend. Between Michael and Hailey, who would I really choose? "I'm sorry," I offered.

Hailey shrugged. "It's okay. I just can't be in a fight with you because I'm failing all my classes and I need your homework help."

"Really? In the past two days?"

"Kind of. All this reading and writing we had due yesterday. It's just not my thing."

I flashed back to the dad asking the question about reading levels at the PTA meeting. I wondered what Pfeiffer was doing to support the kids who needed help.

"Have you told your teachers? I mean, I'm happy to help, but maybe you need tutoring or something."

Hailey nodded. "I'm getting it. I just hate doing the work on my own."

I felt bad. We usually did homework together. "I'll tell you what. Why don't we meet at the library after school today and I will help you."

Hailey nodded. "I have soccer at four thirty."

"Okay, so from three to four fifteen then."

"Great. Thanks so much, Sam!" Hailey moved her books aside and gave me a big hug.

"See you then," I said, glad to be friends again.

"Bye!" Hailey practically skipped away. I guess she was relieved too. *Peace Achieved by Warring Factions.*

Now I just had to cram in rewriting my whole curriculum article (which should have been done by now!), doing my homework, helping Hailey with hers, finalizing the soccer tryout article, oh yeah . . . and writing the Dear Know-It-All column!

I hurried off to class, purposely taking the long way so I wouldn't run into Trigger on the way.

How was I going to get it all done?

Chapter 15

BEST FRIEND TO THE RESCUE

★ ★ ★

The library was almost empty, I guess 'cause it was kind of an Indian summer and people could still enjoy the day once they left school. I found Hailey immediately, and after bumping my chair really hard against my leg (Why, why was I such a klutz?), I settled in beside her and helped her with her work.

One thing about Hailey is that she's a hard worker. She might have some learning differences, but she never gives up, even though lots of stuff takes twice as long for her as for regular learners like me. I was patient with her and we got through her first assignment pretty quick. While she worked on the final part, I pulled out my draft of the article and reread it to see where I could make changes t cut all the "work in progress" stuff.

I guess I sighed hard as I was reading and puzzling, so Hailey said, "What's the matter?"

I tried to blow it off but ended up telling her the whole story, kind of the short version.

"So you have to rewrite the whole thing just because you can't prove that he said that, even though you know he did?"

I nodded miserably.

"Bummer. Bad enough to have to write it once, but twice?"

I half smiled. It would be Hailey's worst nightmare. She turned back to her paper and I kept reading, struggling.

But suddenly, after a couple of minutes, she turned to me. "You've watched the videotape of the meeting, right?"

"What?" My pulse quickened. "What videotape?" Could there be such a thing?

"Well, I'm pretty sure they tape all those meetings. I mean, I remember when my mom was the assistant head of the PTA, she always got dressed up to go to the meetings because she said they film them, and she wanted to look her best."

My jaw dropped. "Who is 'they'?"

"The school."

I looked around. "Where do you think they store the films?"

Hailey shrugged. "Here?" Her palms were up and she swiveled her head around.

I jumped out of my chair, banging my leg again, and quickly crossed the room to the librarian's office. I tapped on her door. "Mrs. Osborne? Excuse me?"

"Hi, honey," Mrs. Osborne was a very kind, grandmotherly woman with white hair, and smart. If you were making a librarian from scratch, she is what you'd dream up. "What can I help you find today?"

I explained what I needed, and before I was even finished, she was nodding her head. "Certainly. The school stores it on the website. It's in the public domain. I can show you how to access it from one of the desktop computers," she said.

"Great. Thanks." Wow! Inside I was bursting with excitement. I followed her to the computer area, pumping my fist at Hailey in victory, but knowing this was just step one. If we found the film, I still had to review the whole thing and see if he said it.

"Here we go." Mrs. Osborne sat down and fiddled with the computer, setting it all up. "Let's see, last Thursday, I believe it was? That was September sixteenth . . ." She clicked on a link and it opened a QuickTime video screen. "Here we go, honey. Let me know if you have any problems."

It was that easy!

"Thanks so much, Mrs. Osborne! You're the best!" Eagerly, I sat down and put on the earphones and began playing the movie. It covered the whole two hour meeting so I tried to fast-forward, but it skipped too much. Finally I just gave up and settled in to watch the whole thing through. At least I knew it would be in the first half of the meeting, before Michael had left, because he said he'd heard it too.

After a while, Hailey came over and tapped me on the shoulder. "I have to go," she said quietly. "Thanks for your help. I'll call you later."

I waved and continued watching. It was really pretty boring, watching this all over again in real time. Finally we got to the part where I was asking questions. I winced. It was horrible watching myself. I had been a little aggressive. Michael was right. Maybe a softer approach would be more appropriate. I kind of looked like a show-off. . . .

Wait! I'd heard it! There it was! I clicked on the rewind button and moved the film back a few frames.

". . . It's kind of a work in progress . . ." Mr. Pfeiffer was saying. Eureka! I jumped up to celebrate, forgetting that I had the earphones on. The cord yanked my head back as I stood up and I kind of cracked my head on the monitor. I looked around. Thank goodness no one was here to see that!

Mrs. Osborne came over to where I was seated. "I'll be going now, unless you need anything else? The custodian will be in shortly to lock up."

"I'll head out with you. Let me just grab my stuff."

It was late for me when I got home. I quickly called Michael Lawrence's house (Daring *me*! Twice in one week!), but his mom, who was superfriendly on the phone, said he wasn't home from practice yet. I couldn't feel totally settled until I'd told him about the video I'd seen. I rushed through my homework and wolfed down my dinner, then I ran back to my computer to tighten up the article.

While I was reviewing it, I got an e-mail from Allie. I had tons of e-mail but hadn't had a chance to sift through them yet today. Allie's said, "R U in a fight with H?"

Is my sister psychic? How does she know everything?

"What?" I wrote back. "Why do you care?"

"Haven't seen her over here in a while. Morgan has a crush on her brother and I don't want it to be awkward if I invite him over for Wii this weekend."

I thought about this for a minute. Allie and her friends socializing with Hailey's brother. Oh, whatever.

"No, it's fine," I typed back. "Not sure why you couldn't stand up and come ask me in my room."

There was no reply, naturally.

"I guess you have all the school supplies you need," I typed. "Or you'd have already been in here." Ha! I love having the last word!

I scrolled through the rest of my e-mail (mostly spam and junk) until my eye caught one from Mr. Trigg! Oh no!

I almost didn't want to open it, but I had to. It read:

"Ms. Martone, I am very sorry, but if I do not

have your column in hand by tomorrow morning, I'm afraid I will have to ask one of your peers to take over. I still think you are the right person for the job, so please do your best to prove it.

Many thanks.

Nathan Trigg"

One of my peers! That could be Michael! Then he'd be on the road to editor in chief! No way!

I started to draft a reply but suddenly an e-mail pinged into my box with all kinds of urgent red flags and exclamation points attached. It was from Hailey. I opened it.

"Major Buddybook meltdown!" it said. "Get on quick and look!"

I groaned. I didn't have time for this junk tonight. I deleted the e-mail, but another one popped up from her, all urgent and desperate again. "It's all about your article! Quick!"

What?

The fastest thing to do was use Allie's account. I ran down the hall and banged on her door as I opened it.

"Sheesh!" she said. She was on her bed, typing

on her phone. She looked annoyed at me, but I was too frantic to care.

"Can I use your Buddybook account?" I asked, breathless.

"Be my guest, desperado. What's up? More hot Michael Lawrence photos just posted?"

"Very funny." I dashed to her computer and went to the sign-in page.

"What's your password?" I asked.

"As if," said Allie. She got off her bed huffily and came to type it in herself. "Look away," she instructed.

But she did quickly help me find what I was looking for. It was the page Michael had created asking people if they were for or against the new curriculum. Lots of people had voted (still more *for* it than *against*, but the numbers had climbed since this morning. It was now 892 for and 412 against). But the problem was the posts. People had been putting up comments and they were growing more and more heated. I couldn't believe my eyes! People were name-calling and it had deteriorated into just a really ugly war.

"Oh my goodness," I said.

"It's like a social revolution," said Allie breathlessly, reading over my shoulder.

"I have to call Michael again!"

"You go girl!" Allie shouted after me, laughing.

I flew back to my room and dialed his number. He answered this time on the second ring.

"I know, I know!" he said, before I could say anything. "I'm taking it down!"

"Wow. You really . . ." I didn't know what to say. "You really started a revolution!"

"I didn't mean to," he said sheepishly. "I shouldn't have had an area for people to post comments. That was my mistake."

"Live and learn," I said, giggling. "I just hope old Pfeiff didn't see it."

"Me too," said Michael. "I was going to call you back once I got this under control," he said.

"Wait!" I said, and told him about what I found in the library.

"That's great news about the video! How did you ever think of such a brilliant thing?" he asked.

I paused. Here was a chance to let him really think I was great, and I hated to miss the opportunity. But to tell him the truth would have him thinking Hailey was great, and I wasn't so psyched about that.

"Sam? What gave you the idea?"

Mr. Trigg had said, "All's fair in love and war. . . ."

Martone Betrays Best Friend over a Guy.

"Are you still there? Sam?"

Darn it! I couldn't do it. "Stick to the facts, kid," I heard my journalism teacher Mr. Bloom saying. Stick to the facts.

"It was Hailey!" I blurted finally.

"What was Hailey?" asked Michael.

"She was the one who knew that they tape the PTA meetings. Her mom used to be in the PTA. She was the one who thought to ask in the library. And they had it. It was all her idea."

"Wow! Hailey really saved the day!" said Michael.

I winced. Oh well, I thought. There goes my chance at love.

"Looks like you're as good at picking friends as you are at everything else!" said Michael cheerily.

What?

Did he really just say that? I didn't know how

to reply. I looked at the receiver in my hand. Did Michael Lawrence really think I was good at things? Like what, I desperately wanted to ask. List some things, please!

"Oh, uh . . . thanks?" I stammered.

"Listen, this is all good, but I've gotta run. Let's swap drafts one more time before the end of the night via e-mail. Then I'll meet you at the *Voice* tomorrow and we can file the story together, okay? Give me your e-mail address since you're not on Buddybook."

"Okay." I hesitated. "Newsysam1" sounded so cute when I chose it. Now it was just one more embarrassment.

"Uh, Sam? Your e-mail?"

"Oh, right!" I said, and gave it to him.

Michael chuckled. "Bye, Pasty! I mean *Newsy*!" Ugh.

I replaced the receiver in the cradle and looked at the phone for a long time. Then I wrapped my arms around myself and hugged my shoulders. Hailey had said it: at least I had nicknames. Maybe that meant something. I felt all warm inside. I think I might actually have a chance with Michael Lawrence!

Impulsively I picked up the receiver again and dialed Hailey. She really was a great friend.

"You're the best!" I said when she picked up.

"Thanks!"

"You saved my butt today!"

"Well you saved mine with the first-person narrative paper!"

"Oh, that was nothing!"

"We're a good team," said Hailey.

I smiled. "We are."

After we hung up, I trudged up the stairs to my room and settled back at my desk. I put a few lines in the article about the Buddybook war, and polished up a few other things, then I sent it to Michael and also posted a copy to the *Voice*'s server so I could work on it there tomorrow.

Then I pulled out the manila folder from behind my desk, opened it up, and started to type.

"Dear Unlucky," I began, and my fingers flew over the keys with all I had to say.

Chapter 16

LUCKY IN LOVE?

Well, I made the deadlines. Both of them.

Michael and I got our article all polished up, of course, even though we both got yelled at by our moms for staying up so late e-mailing. Mr. Trigg was really pleased with it and very impressed by our reporting.

"Mr. Lawrence, quite brilliant to research the funding. Jolly good idea!" he said. "And Ms. Martone, the video evidence is compelling. Very cloak and dagger."

"It wasn't my idea, but I'm glad I got the lead. I can't reveal my source."

"Sources are what make journalism go round, my girl!"

"And friends!" I added.

"Thanks," said Michael, smiling at me.

Oh dear. I hadn't meant him, of course, but now I realized I should have. It was pretty cute that he thought of me as a friend. It's a good first step to major romance, I think. At least that's what I told Unlucky Taste in my Dear Know-It-All column.

"Yeah, I think we both learned a lot doing this," I said.

Mr. Trigg was nodding happily. "Excellent. Like what?"

Michael and I smiled at each other. "Well . . ." I began. "You have to listen when you ask questions. You can't just keep firing them off, and you can't always rely on just copying down answers. You've got to really hear what people are saying . . ."

"And you've got to be careful of social media," added Michael.

"Certainly, we've seen that all over the world," said Mr. Trigg, all serious now.

"And you've got to try to look at both sides of everything . . ." I said.

"Yeah, and also the gray areas and the works in

progress in between," Michael chimed in. "Also, you have to remember to feed Sam and stay out of her way."

I elbowed him. "Be quiet!" But he knew I wasn't mad. We were friends. I was starting to feel a lot more comfortable around him. And he was still so super cute. "Anyway, as long as you're making cinnamon buns, I'm ready to eat," I added.

Mr. Trigg looked back and forth between us, smiling like a proud father. "Maybe we have a new arrangement next year. Co-editors-in-chief!" He tapped his chin thoughtfully with his index finger. "Yes, like a Hepburn and Tracy movie. I can just see it . . ." He wandered back to his desk, lost in thought.

Michael and I watched him go and then burst out laughing. "Whatever!" he said.

"Co-editors-in-chief—as if!" I said, but Michael knew I was joking.

"Good job, partner," said Michael, reaching out his hand to shake mine.

I placed my hand in his large, warm paw and we shook, smiling. "A pleasure doing business with you, Pasty," he said.

"Thanks, Mikey."

The paper came out the following Monday and there was a ton of hoopla. Mr. Pfeiffer called Mr. Trigg and yelled about being misquoted, but Mr. Trigg said he was standing by his staff and directed Mr. Pfeiffer to watch the video on the school website. That shut him up fast.

Hailey and I were at lunch together when she opened the paper for the first time. I held my breath as she read my cover story (Front page! Top of the fold!).

"Sammy, this is awesome!" she said, and she dove across the table to give me a huge hug. "Even though I don't understand half of it!" She laughed.

"Thanks!" I said, my voice muffled by her shoulder.

I finished my lunch while she flipped through the rest of the pages, chattering and commenting on everything. Finally, she got to the back inside cover. The Dear Know-It-All page. I looked at her face while she started to read, but then I felt like I was invading her privacy and I had to get away.

"Want anything? I'm going up for dessert," I said.

Hailey didn't even look up. "No thanks. I'm good," she said, riveted by the paper.

I watched her from afar as I gathered up my chocolate cake. Out of the corner of my eye, I spied Michael walking in with Jeff Perry. Oops. I didn't want to be chatting with him when she finished reading. I quickly dashed back to my table and slid into my seat.

Hailey had finished reading and looked startled by my reentry.

"Everything okay?" she asked. "You looked like you were being chased."

"Yeah, I'm fine. You?"

"Yeah." She looked at me strangely. "Why wouldn't I be?"

Oh goodness! I have to be careful! "Oh nothing. Just being polite!" Yikes. "Can I see the Dear Know-It-All?"

"Sure. Here." She slid it over to me. I looked out of the corner of my eye for any signs of emotion, one way or the other, but Hailey's face didn't betray anything.

I bent my head and began to read what only Mr. Trigg and I knew I'd written.

Dear Unlucky,

You have done nothing wrong. The people we choose as our friends are the people we have the most in common with, so it's no surprise that you and your best friend like the same person. In this case, I would say honesty is the best policy. You should tell your best friend how you feel. There is no "wrong or right" in this situation. Not everything is black or white; there is always a gray area to consider. If your friend is really your friend, then he or she will wish you all the best, and if it works out with the person you like, then your friend will be happy for you. That's how I would feel if you were my friend.

Love is not fact based. It's not something we can shut down when it gets out of our control, like a page on Buddybook. It's just what happens when all the pieces fall into place. Good luck to you and your friend, and the person you both like. I hope it all works out for the best.

Your friend,
Dear Know-It-All

I finished reading and I looked up at Hailey. "Wow." My voice was kind of scratchy so I cleared my throat. "Great column." I looked around the cafeteria and noticed the kids at every table gathered around copies of the *Voice*. Were they reading my article? Were they reading my column? It was a weird feeling, but a great one.

"Sam," Hailey began. Her voice was serious. "I... I have a confession to make. I wrote this letter. I ... I had a crush on Michael Lawrence."

"Hey, dudes!" Jeff Perry clattered his tray onto the table and sat down, with Michael Lawrence right behind him.

"What's up, ladies?" said Michael.

Hailey and I looked at each other and started to laugh. Hard.

Michael winced. "Was it something we said?"

I felt bad. He was embarrassed, but I didn't want him to feel that way. "No, totally not. It is not about you at all. We're just laughing about my stupid sister, Allie. She's obsessed with texting, that's all." I lied quickly so no one's feelings would be hurt. Only a friend could tell you something you needed to hear.

Hailey told me I hadn't been so nice to Michael, so it was about time I started listening.

Michael relaxed and smiled back. "Oh. Got it."

I really needed to talk to Hailey, and as much as I (we?) loved Michael, I had to leave and finish my conversation with her. "Guys, hate to eat and run, but . . ."

"We just got here!" protested Jeff. "And we have all this great stuff in the *Voice* to talk about!

Hailey was standing up and gathering her tray and things and I followed suit.

"Sorry, boys! Sometimes girls just need to be alone! Adios." I waggled my fingers at them.

"Hey! Got something for you!" said Michael. He reached into the front pocket of his jeans and pulled out a scrap of white paper. "Here. Open it later. It's about the paper." He handed it to me.

I looked down but didn't open it. "Okay. Thanks! See you guys!"

Hailey was waiting for me at the door.

She kept right on talking as if we hadn't been interrupted, the words tumbling out of her in a great torrent. "What I wanted to say was . . . I'm over it. The crush. I'm so sorry. I just . . . I guess I felt comfortable around him and I was used to checking him out, you know, on your behalf. It was like I just talked myself into it. But now . . . I mean, this past week . . . I see how you two are perfect for each other. I mean, you share all these interests, and he's so in love with you . . . and . . ."

"Wait, wait. Stop. Slow down. Okay. Wait. *What?*"

"Michael Lawrence. I had a crush. It's over. Anyway, he loves you."

"He does not!" I said. But I couldn't stop the small smile that lifted the corners of my mouth. "Do you think?"

"Duh! Stealing your notebook, inviting you over, baking you cinnamon buns for goodness' sake! And the way he looks at you!"

"Wait, you think he stole my notebook?"

"Totally."

"Huh." I hadn't thought of that. But the cinnamon buns had given me pause.

"Anyway, I still do think he's a really great guy, and I think you should be a lot nicer to him. He really likes you."

"Wow. I'd never thought of it that way. Thanks Hails. You're the best. And . . . and . . . well, I'm sorry if you liked him too. I guess that was kind of hard."

Hailey shrugged and hugged me tight and ran off to her next class. *All's Well That Ends Well.*

I went to the bathroom, and after I'd washed and dried my hands, I pulled Michael's note out of my pocket.

"Great column, Pasty," it said. Awww. Wait. Which column was he talking about? Our column? Or Know-It-All? Oh my gosh. Did Michael Lawrence *know*?

Oh boy.

After school the staff met at the *Cherry Valley Voice* office to go over our first edition. Everyone was talking and laughing and was in a good mood. Everyone at school had been buzzing about the paper, and there was a rumor that the PTA was going to talk about our article at the next meeting. Holy cow!

"Silence!" called Mr. Trigg. "Silence, people, please!"

Everyone settled down.

"First," said Mr. Trigg, "I'd like to commend you all on one fabulous first edition of the paper. Excellent start!"

Everyone started clapping and cheering. "I believe our stalwart editor in chief, Susannah, would like to address the troops now."

Susannah stood up. "Well, ditto to what Mr. Trigg said. Plus I'd like to call out a few special people who did some great work. Jeff Perry's photos were fantastic." Everyone clapped. Jeff looked really happy.

"And Michael Lawrence and Samantha Martone's story really set the tone for the year. It was great journalism!" I was so proud, but also a little shy. Michael high-fived me. "It was good teamwork!" he called out. I knew I was smiling really, really hard. It felt like my face might crack, and I wasn't even wearing a mud mask!

"And," said Susannah, "I'd like to thank all the columnists who also got the year off to such a strong start, including a really great and thoughtful Know-It-All column, whoever he or she may be. It was kind and good advice, and I'm sure it helped a lot of people."

"That's true," whispered Michael, leaning in.

"Um . . . what?" I asked.

"That it was a great column," he whispered back. I looked at him. Was he just saying that or did he know?

"Yeah," I said. "It must have been pretty hard to write."

"Or be in that situation," said Michael. "It takes a really good friend to write something like that."

"Oh, that too," I said. Now I was really confused. Boys. Just when you think you've figured them out.

Susannah was going over assignments for next week with Mr. Trigg. I was still trying to figure out if Michael knew that I was Know-It-All.

"So what do you say, Pasty?" said Michael.

"Um . . . what?"

Michael rolled his eyes. "You and me as a writing team for the next story? I don't know how we'll top this first one but . . ."

"Oh!" I said. "Oh, sure. Yes! That would be so great!" Then I stopped and laughed. "You know, Hailey wondered why they didn't overhaul the lunch menu before the curriculum." I don't know why I said that. Maybe I was still thinking of Hailey a little bit. Plus she was sure helping me out with stories.

"Hey!" said Michael. "That's it! That's our next story! Why the tuna surprise is not a good surprise! It's going to be groundbreaking journalism." He put his arm around me. It felt really, really nice.

I laughed. I didn't know if he was kidding or not. I just knew that I really loved him right then and there, even if I didn't know if he felt the same way. And that the next time he invited me over for a cinnamon bun, I was definitely accepting.

Journalist Keeps Best Friend, Gains 500 Pounds on All–Cinnamon-Bun Diet. And Is Still in Love.